P9-DFC-326

MURDER

IN THE

LINCOLN

BEDROOM

ALSO BY ELLIOTT ROOSEVELT

Murder in Georgetown
Murder in the Map Room
Murder at Midnight
Murder in the Château
Murder in the Executive Mansion
A Royal Murder
Murder in the East Room
New Deal for Death
Murder in the West Wing
Murder in the Red Room
The President's Man
A First-Class Murder
Murder in the Blue Room
Murder in the Rose Garden
Murder in the Oval Office
Murder at the Palace
The White House Pantry Murder
Murder at Hobcaw Barony
The Hyde Park Murder
Murder and the First Lady

Perfect Crimes (ed.)

MURDER
IN THE
LINCOLN
BEDROOM

An Eleanor Roosevelt Mystery

Elliott Roosevelt

THOMAS DUNNE BOOKS
St. Martin's Minotaur
New York

THOMAS DUNNE BOOKS.
An imprint of St. Martin's Press.

ISBN 0-312-26150-0

White House—Second Floor, Center Part—1943

South

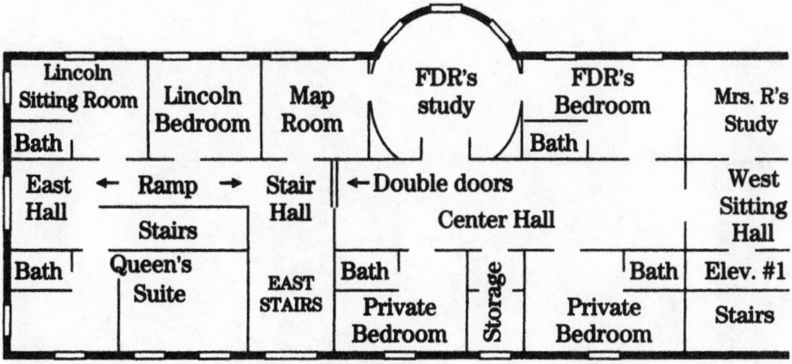

Lincoln Sitting Room
Lincoln Bedroom
Map Room
FDR's study
FDR's Bedroom
Mrs. R's Study
Bath
Bath
East Hall
← Ramp →
Stair Hall
← Double doors
Center Hall
West Sitting Hall
Stairs
Bath
Queen's Suite
EAST STAIRS
Bath
Private Bedroom
Storage
Bath
Private Bedroom
Elev. #1
Stairs

North

MURDER
IN THE
LINCOLN
BEDROOM

I

May 1943

MRS. ROOSEVELT STOOD AT a window in her study and watched cars arrive. She had been downstairs at 2:00 A.M. to welcome Prime Minister Winston Churchill and his daughter Sarah to the White House. The Chief of the Imperial General Staff, Field Marshal Alan Brooke, had flown on a separate plane and arrived half an hour later. When these guests had been installed in their rooms, the First Lady had gone to bed.

Now she watched General George Marshall arrive, then Admiral Ernest King. They came to the White House often, and she knew both of them well. The man she was really curious about was the last to arrive: General Dwight David Eisenhower. It was generally assumed that General Marshall would command the forces that would invade France and that General Eisenhower would replace General Marshall as Chief of Staff. That was why he was here: to take part in the discussions leading to major decisions and so be better ready to take Marshall's job when the new appointments were made. Mrs. Roosevelt had met Eisenhower when he was a major, serving as aide de camp to General MacArthur, and she wondered how the years and his rapid promotion had changed him.

He was accompanied by his English driver and bridge partner, Kay Summersby. They had flown all the way from Algiers.

That General Eisenhower had Miss Summersby with him was suggestive. Almost no one in Washington had the least idea who the handsome young woman might be, but the President and Mrs. Roosevelt had heard the rumor, which was current in London, that Miss Summersby was the general's bed partner and that he had indicated to General Marshall that he intended to seek a divorce from his wife so he could marry Miss Summersby.

Mrs. Roosevelt detested gossip, and she discounted this heavily; but she could not help but be curious about the charming young Englishwoman, a former actress, who accompanied General Eisenhower wherever he went.

The plan had been that the Prime Minister would occupy the Queen's Bedroom suite, in which he had been comfortable before, and that General Eisenhower would occupy the Lincoln Bedroom suite. Word had come from the general, however, that he wanted a two-bedroom suite on the third floor, where his presence—and Miss Summersby's presence, too, as Mrs. Roosevelt surmised—

would far less likely be noticed. The Trident Conference was so secret that almost no one knew that the Prime Minister and the Chief of the Imperial General Staff were in the United States. Even Mrs. Eisenhower did not know that General Eisenhower was in Washington.

White House security had abruptly become tighter. Mrs. Roosevelt, who'd had to learn to live with wartime protection, felt constricted by the extremely heavy shield that had dropped around the executive mansion this week. She understood why. She could not and did not complain. But the pervasive and ominous presence of soldiers and extra Secret Service agents in and around the house lay like a half-smothering blanket.

Security had been tight since 1941. But this— Since the participants would *fly* back across the Atlantic, the very fact they were not in London had to be kept secret, lest the Nazis increase their air patrols and lie in wait for the returning conferees. The conference would not last long. Before the end of the month things would again be as close to normal as anything could be during a war. And Mrs. Roosevelt would be a little more comfortable with that.

That May the cherry trees blossomed in Washington, as they did every year. Because they were Japanese cherry trees—in fact, the original ones had been a gift from the emperor of Japan—a few zealots thought it would be a patriotic act to cut them down. Despite this feverish nationalism, the profusion of pink cherry blossoms lent

Washington an appearance of continuity it did not have in many other places. World War II was in its second year for America, and the capitol city was a very different place from what it had been before December, 1941.

Beginning in March, 1933, a little more than ten years ago, the invasion of New Dealers had begun. The *old* Washingtonians, the ones who had been there a century or more, were called the Cave Dwellers, even by so discreet a publication as the *Saturday Evening Post.* They had been shocked by the professors and social workers of the New Deal, who did not know how to dress for dinner. They had been dismayed by the degradation of mores, disgusted by the apparel, manners, and conversation of the "new people." Alice Roosevelt Longworth, daughter of President Theodore Roosevelt, who had been married in the White House, was a caustic commentator on this subject.

But if that had shocked and dismayed them, they had been totally unprepared for what war brought.

The Cave Dwellers had never thought to see the day when the streets of their city would throng with young women wearing *trousers!* Trousers, yes—called slacks—with no hats, their hair confined only in snoods, if at all. When they did wear skirts, their legs were bare! And it wasn't only that. As part of a campaign to save fabrics, their skirts were short, in some instances hardly covering their knees. They wore bright-red lipstick and rouged their cheeks. They smoked cigarettes, even on the streets, and tossed the butts in the gutters. Whiskey was in short supply, but these young women in trousers drank it when they could get it.

Government Girls, they were called.

No wonder young men liked them. It was reported that they had loose morals. They looked as if they did.

And the young men! Virtually every one wore a uniform of some sort. A few were officers, but most of them were just young men of one sort or another, many of the kind once to be found in the Civilian Conservation Corps camps—boys of no family background particularly, no university background particularly, no prospects particularly, no distinction particularly. Faceless and just passing through. Temporary.

Everything was temporary. People. Work. Agencies. Buildings. Washington had become a temporary city. How could newcomers learn manners and standards and fit themselves into the elegant lifestyle the city had once had when they had come unexpectedly, many unwillingly, and were expected to stay only a short time?

New Dealers had marred the beauty of the Tidal Basin by throwing up a monument to Thomas Jefferson, completed and dedicated only now, in the spring of 1943. Critics said of it that it was surrounded by so many columns that they formed a cage for the statue of Jefferson inside.

Ugly temporary wooden buildings had sprung up everywhere, even on The Mall.

The lights did not come on at night. The Capitol dome,

the Washington Monument, and other buildings that had glowed for decades in electric light now stood gloomy and dark. In fact, some nights the city blacked out—that is, turned off all outdoor lights and drew heavy black curtains across the windows of lighted rooms.

The Gayety Burlesque flourished. A Washington institution that had been attended every time the show changed by no less a figure than Justice Oliver Wendell Holmes, was now filled every night with raucous young men in uniform who demanded that the strippers take off more and more. And they did, until there was no more to take off. The vice squad, which had once carefully monitored these performances, turned away. It would have been unpatriotic to deny the GIs their fun.

The military presence was oppressive, particularly the anti-aircraft batteries that stood in parks and were mounted on the roofs of buildings. Even the White House grounds sprouted anti-aircraft batteries surrounded by heaps of sandbags. Lighter batteries were mounted on the White House roof.

It was a frustrating time to be a Cave Dweller. It was a sad but fascinating time to be Mrs. Roosevelt. She had three sons in the service, all of them at risk in combat zones. It was inspiring to watch her husband, the President, shoulder unprecedented responsibilities and strive to win what had at first seemed an all but unwinnable war. She tried to help him in every way she could.

She could not help but observe that the unyielding demands of global war imposed a burden on him that would have staggered a man in perfect health. But of course he was not a man in perfect health. The vigorous, exuberant young man she had married had been brought to a wheelchair by infantile paralysis. He had lost more than the use of his legs. He did not know that Dr. McIntyre let her see the diagnoses he made. The truth was that Franklin D. Roosevelt was suffering from heart problems that would have sent another man to a sedentary life.

Today, she knew, she could help him best by keeping all distractions away from him, to the extent that such a thing was possible. She had a great many things on her mind—the way Negroes were treated in the armed forces, smoldering dissatisfaction among the nation's coal miners, decent housing for the Government Girls, among many others—but she was resolved to say nothing of any of these things to the President during this secret Trident Conference.

His problems— Well, she was not prepared to say they were immeasurably more important than the problems she had in mind; but she was entirely ready to say they were immeasurably more urgent.

She didn't know every decision that needed to be taken at this conference. She suspected that among them were these—

—When would the Allies open a Second Front? The President and the Prime Minister were under unrelenting pressure from Premier Stalin to launch an invasion of Western Europe. Even if it failed and was thrown back, it would relieve the pressure on the Soviet Union, which was threatening to crack. The numbers of casualties Russia had suffered amounted to several times those the other Allies had suffered, and if it collapsed, the entire might of the German military machine would turn west and probably launch an overpowering invasion of the British Isles.

The invasion of North Africa had been a gimmick in Stalin's eyes. As he saw it, only minimal British and American forces had been engaged, while his country bled.

Sicily, Italy. These meant nothing. When would there be an invasion of *France?* Only that would relieve the crushing pressure on the Soviet Union.

—On the other hand, from the British and American point of view, must there be an invasion of France at all? There were two alternatives. First, the air-power people believed that Germany could be defeated from the skies. The Eighth Air Force and the RAF were taking major losses from German fighters and anti-aircraft fire; and yet their generals asserted that Germany could not much longer withstand the round-the-clock bombing. Second, Churchill postulated attacking what he called the "soft underbelly of the Axis"—meaning, attacking in the Balkans.

—If there were to be a Cross-Channel invasion, who would command? The British, who had far more experience of combat in this war than the Americans, thought

General Montgomery should command. Since America would be providing the bulk of the men and materiél, the Americans took the attitude that an American should command.

—If it were to be an American, then who? Everyone assumed it would be General Marshall. The President had a different idea. He felt he needed Marshall in Washington, where his superb organizational skills and his all-but-infallible advice would be irreplaceable. The President leaned toward General Eisenhower—which was why he was here for the Trident Conference.

In addition to these major problems, the conference had to face difficulties in the North Atlantic, where U-boats seemed to sink Allied vessels almost at will, plus major problems in the Pacific, where the astounding American victory at Midway, a year before, had perhaps doomed Japan—except that Japan didn't know it yet.

The conference met chiefly in the oval Diplomatic Reception Room on the ground floor of the White House, a room chosen because it was adjacent to the Situation Room or Map Room and had a connecting door to that room. During Winston Churchill's first visit to the White House, in 1941, he had suggested to the President that he should have a special secret room where the latest reports could be constantly assembled into a situation report to which the Commander-in-Chief could refer at any time. This advice culminated in the Situation Room, its walls permanently covered with maps, with markers stuck in to show the position of forces on any given day.

Mrs. Roosevelt went down to see to it that arrangements had been made to keep the conferees supplied with coffee and tea, also pastries. Mr. Churchill would require a sip of brandy now and again during the morning, and she had told Mrs. Nesbitt to see that he had it.

In the Center Hall she encountered General Eisenhower. If she hadn't already known him, she would not have been able to recognize him by his clothes. He was in mufti—as was Field Marshall Brooke, she would soon see. His somewhat ill-fitting gray suit was intended, apparently, to disguise him, and to some extent it did.

"Mrs. Roosevelt. It is an honor."

He was still Major Eisenhower, broad and bland of face but with an engaging wide grin.

"My congratulations to you, General. You have done very well since I saw you last."

"Thank you."

The door to the conference room was open, and he obviously did not want to enter late, so he nodded, grinned again, and hurried into the meeting.

She saw all the conferees at the President's cocktail hour, held as always in the West Sitting Hall on the second floor. Admiral King was not there. All the others were, with Sarah Churchill and Kay Summersby. General Edwin "Pa" Watson, the President's military aide, was there, too.

In past years Missy LeHand, the faithful secretary, had

sat at the President's side and helped him mix his cocktails. She had never ceased to be amused by the way Franklin Roosevelt mixed his martinis: with the ceremony and precision of a pharmacist filling a prescription—though she herself never drank them, preferring and drinking whiskey. She was not there this evening. She was in the hospital, and Mrs. Roosevelt knew the President suspected he would never see her again.

Sarah Churchill wore a bright spring frock. She drank and smoked and was obviously little impressed by the ranks of the men around her. The story was told that she had been intimately friendly—not perhaps erotically friendly—with the erstwhile King Edward VIII, during his years as Prince of Wales, before he became enamored with Wallis Warfield Simpson. She had been friendly enough that she dared call him Sixy—because he had six names: Albert Christian George Andrew Patrick David.

Dear old David Lloyd George often put an arm around her waist and hugged her, and she called him Taffy, because he was Welsh and in reference to the old English doggerel verse:

Taffy was a Welshman,
Taffy was a thief.
Taffy came to our house
And stole a piece of beef.

No one else would have dared lay that one on Lloyd George, but Sarah did, and he laughed at it.

Kay Summersby had arrived at the White House in uniform, but it was the uniform of an enlisted rank, and tonight she wore a simple gray knit dress. She was quiet and deferential.

The First Lady had a speaking engagement at a dinner outside the White House, and she stopped at the cocktail party only briefly. It was one of the President's chief pleasures, and she had a sense that, no matter how hard she tried not to, she dampened these little occasions. She was a jolly person, not a somber one, but she was not the cocktail-party type. She knew it and left her husband to enjoy himself, usually with a few friends, tonight with dignitaries.

She sipped a glass of sherry and heard the Prime Minister say—"But what will it cost us . . . in blood and treasure . . . to subdue *this* fellow in his turn? If we leave *him* hegemonist on the Continent, what shall we have . . . *gained?*"

She knew what he meant: that he held Joseph Stalin in no higher regard than he held Adolf Hitler.

She knew the President did not agree, that *he* thought that when the Nazis were defeated and the Soviets relieved of the threat of annihilation, Stalin could be convinced to enter into a permanent alliance based on peace and justice.

The President did not rise to the challenge.

General Marshall did. "If Germany defeats the Soviet Union, what will it cost in blood and treasure to —I believe your words were something like these—erase the stain of Hitlerism from the world?"

General Eisenhower, conspicuously aware of being hugely outranked here, listened gravely and said almost nothing. Kay Summersby was more at ease than he was, probably because she knew she was not expected to say anything. Sarah Churchill exchanged quiet pleasantries with her, on the side.

Kay Summersby was an exceptionally handsome woman: tall and slender and graceful, cheerful and vivacious. She was a typical English blond and had been a model and actress before the war. She had been engaged to be married to a young army officer, but he had been killed. It would have required no more than having her as his driver and companion to generate the rumors that linked her romantically to General Eisenhower, and Mrs. Roosevelt was much inclined to dismiss the gossip.

It was apparent that he wanted to be closer to her. From time to time, when one of the others said something, he would nod at Kay, as if to say, "Remember that; it's important, and we'll want to talk about it." Another rumor about the pair was that he placed a great deal of confidence in her and was often influenced by her judgments on political and diplomatic matters.

Mrs. Roosevelt had met Sarah Churchill in France in the spring of 1941, during her secret mission to Vichy France. Sarah had represented her father at that meeting. She was a beautiful young woman with auburn hair and green eyes. Her personal life had been an annoyance for her father, who had once sent her brother Randolph to the United States to try to persuade her not to marry a Viennese music-hall comedian twice her age and reputed to be a Jew. A London newspaper reported of her that she had appeared on stage as a chorus girl, "as nearly naked as the law allows." The First Lady remembered her as smart and brave.

Committed to a dinner meeting, Mrs. Roosevelt left the Trident conferees, knowing that their cocktail hour would be followed by a brief dinner and a return to their weighty deliberations.

II

MRS. ROOSEVELT RETURNED TO the White House a little after eleven on a rainy evening. Even accompanied by three Secret Service attendants, she had to work her way through the tedium of the new security—grasping about in the dark, the mansion being blacked out. Inside, the building was lighted as it had been since the war began—though rather dimly as compared to peacetime, to save electricity—and the windows were covered with heavy blackout curtains. The place was far more cheerful during the day, when the curtains were drawn back and daylight was allowed to fill the rooms.

She walked through the ground-floor hall. The Trident Conference was still in session in the Diplomatic Reception Room. On impulse, she turned east and started up the stairs, rather than walking on west to the elevator. On the first floor the state rooms—East Room, Blue Room, and so on—were all but dark. She continued up the stairs and arrived at the second floor.

"Ma'am. Excuse me. No one is permitted to enter. We've got the East Hall blocked off."

The man who had spoken was a young, uniformed White House policeman.

The First Lady glared at him. "I don't believe it's blocked against *me*," she said brusquely.

"Ma'am, I'm sorry, but—I have my orders, ma'am, from the Secret Service agent in charge of the investigation."

"And who is that?"

"Agent Szczygiel, ma'am."

"Tell Mr. Szczygiel I want to talk to him."

In a moment Stan Szczygiel—fortunately his name was pronounced "Sea Gull"—came up the ramp between the East Hall and the Stair Hall. He was a veteran agent of the Secret Service. He was in fact seventy-three years old and had been called out of retirement when several of the agents most familiar with the inner White House left to serve in the armed forces. He was a squat, square man, both of face and physique, and perhaps his most memorable feature was his oversize, gin-reddened nose. He and Mrs. Roosevelt were old friends. She had held a retirement party for him and had seen to it that the President did not fail to attend.

"What's going on, Stan? You are aware that Mr. Churchill—"

"Nothing to do with *him*, ma'am. The problem is in the Lincoln Bedroom."

"And what *is* the problem?"

"We have a corpse in there."

Mrs. Roosevelt glanced quickly around. "Mr. Churchill will be coming up to enter the suite across the hall, at any minute. Close the door to the Lincoln Bedroom. Get these extra men out of sight. We don't want Mr. Churchill to know that a body has been found in the bedroom immediately opposite his."

Szczygiel gave the orders, mostly by gestures.

The uniformed officer who had stopped Mrs. Roosevelt lingered uncertainly in the hall.

"What is *his* name? What is he doing?"

"His name is Willoughby, ma'am. He's the man on duty in the hallway between these two suites. Mr. Churchill would have seen him before."

She smiled at the young officer. "Carry on, Willoughby. Carry on," she said lightly.

The body lying on the carpet in the Lincoln Bedroom was that of a slight man, probably in his thirties, dressed in an unbuttoned cream-white double-breasted suit. He lay on his back. His open eyes seemed to stare at the ceiling through his round, gold-rimmed spectacles. Not contorted in death, the face was bland, unmemorable. No wound was visible, but the carpet was bloody. He had died, apparently, of a hard blow to the back of the head.

"Who is he?" asked Mrs. Roosevelt. "I've seen him around here, but I can't place him."

"His name is Paul Weyrich," said Szczygiel. "He

worked in an office on the second floor of the West Wing. I don't know what his duties were, exactly, but he was a lawyer as I understand it. He had full clearance to enter the White House, anyway."

"To enter the residence? Not just the West Wing?"

"Once you are on the grounds and inside," said Szczygiel, "it is not terribly difficult to make your way here and there—particularly if you have been working here for a while and have learned the intricacies of the White House."

"Who found him?"

"Willoughby. He considered it his duty to check into all the rooms in this end from time to time—with the exception of course of Mr. Churchill's room. He opens doors and shines his flashlight around. This was about ten o'clock. It shook him a little to find a corpse."

Mrs. Roosevelt nodded. "I have seen quite of few of them," she said, "but I don't think I shall ever fail to be shaken when I see the silent clay of what was not long before a living human being."

"We've called the DC medical examiner. Do you want Captain Kennelly?"

She nodded. "I think so. Captain Kennelly has proved most effective in every investigation I've ever seen him do. I've every respect for the Secret Service, but your function is guarding, not investigating. I shall make the call. Let no one move the body until Captain Kennelly arrives."

She went to her study at the far end of the second-floor

hall and opened her card file to look for Kennelly's home telephone number. His wife answered the call.

"This is Mrs. Eleanor Roosevelt. I am sorry to disturb Captain Kennelly at this hour, but—"

Mrs. Roosevelt and Ed Kennelly had worked together on investigations for almost as many years as she had lived in the White House. A warm, chaste affection had developed between them, to the extent that sometimes he squeezed her hand or kissed her on the cheek. He had confessed to her once that if their situations had been totally different he would have sought a closer relationship. Very few men had ever said anything like that to her, and she could not help but cherish his friendship.

They were roughly the same age, but otherwise two people could not have been more different. Ed was a rough-hewn Irishman who had worked his way up from beat cop to captain of detectives. He spoke with a brogue. He smoked and he drank. Still, she liked him. More important, she trusted him.

She sat down on the antique rosewood bed that dominated the Lincoln Bedroom. She was aware, as many people weren't, that Abraham Lincoln had never slept in this room, much less in this bed. It had been a cabinet room during his presidency, and he had signed the Emancipation Proclamation in this room. Later it had become a guest room, and the bed had been moved in from another guest room.

Ed's professionalism showed immediately when he knelt beside the body of Paul Weyrich. "This man fell face-first and has been turned over," he said.

"None of our people touched him," said Szczygiel.

"Look at the bruise right here," said Kennelly, pointing at a bruise on the forehead. "Hell, he all but broke his nose." He looked up and spoke to the medical examiners, who had not touched the body either. "Look for bruises on his knees," he said to them. "I'd say he was coldcocked from behind with a sap. He fell forward, probably hit his knees hard, then went down on his face. Then somebody turned him over."

"Why?" asked Mrs. Roosevelt.

"Well . . . his suit jacket is open, which suggests to me that somebody unbuttoned it and took a look inside for something they thought he would be carrying. Which . . . obviously was not that gun."

"What?"

Ed reached inside the jacket and pulled out a .32 caliber Colt automatic: a small black pistol that would fit inside a man's clothes. "Interesting question here, Stan, don't you think? How'd he carry a pistol through today's White House security? The army boys outside even gave *me* a hard time."

"First-class question," Szczygiel agreed solemnly. "But I'm *more* interested in why he was carrying a pistol in the White House. What don't we know about this guy?"

"He was found about ten o'clock," said Mrs. Roosevelt,

"but probably had been dead for some time. Can we guess how long, before the medical examiner works on him and tells us?"

"From the way the blood has dried on the rug," said Kennelly, "I'd guess he's been dead more than three hours."

"I believe we must learn as much as we can as quickly as we can," said Mrs. Roosevelt. "I think it would be entirely appropriate to search his office."

With the exception of the Oval Office itself, offices in the West Wing were far from luxurious. Offices on the second floor were modest indeed. Weyrich had occupied a tiny office just opposite the second-floor men's room. His secretary had an even smaller room. The offices did not connect, and she had to go out in the hall to come to his room.

His furniture had consisted of what the First Lady thought of as government furniture—a yellow-oak desk, scarred all over by cigarette burns. A yellow-oak swivel chair. A gooseneck lamp. A side chair of dark-stained wood that did not match the other furniture. A steel typing table on which sat a Royal portable typewriter. Three wooden filing cabinets. A raincoat, a hat, and an umbrella hung from hooks on the wall. A scrap of threadbare faux Oriental carpet covered about a third of the floor. One narrow, curtainless window looked out on the roof of the colonnade that connected the West Wing to the White House.

Mrs. Roosevelt sat down in the side chair. Ed sat down behind the desk, in the swivel chair, which creaked shrilly.

A humidor half filled with light-colored pipe tobacco shared one corner of the desk with a big round ceramic ashtray and a rack holding four pipes. An ink-stained green desk blotter covered most of the surface. Ed pulled out several of the notes tucked in the corners of the blotter holder and showed them to Mrs. Roosevelt and Szczygiel. They were telephone numbers.

He opened the center drawer of the desk and began to sift through the contents. "Ah-hah," he said immediately. He had found a letter, which he showed to the other two.

Dearest Paul
Please accept this modest little tie clasp as a token of my very great affection. I doubt it is possible for you to love me as I have learned to love you over these past few months, but I mean to express myself the best I can and hope I do not embarrass you. I am yours in whatever way you want me.

With all my love,
Julie

"Who do you suppose Julie is?" Ed asked.

"We must find out," said Mrs. Roosevelt.

"A lover," said Stan. "A lover capable of killing him out of unrequited love. Which doesn't explain why he was carrying a loaded automatic on the second floor of the White House. What was he doing in the Lincoln Bedroom? Suppose he was waiting for a chance to take a shot at Churchill?"

"An address book," said Kennelly, laying a small, leather-covered book on the desk top. He opened it and flipped through. "He had some interesting friends. Father Coughlin. Gerald L. K. Smith. Charles Lindbergh. Colonel Robert McCormick. Some of these other names . . . well, it will be a good idea to check all of them."

"Roosevelt-haters," the First Lady suggested.

Ed nodded. "Isolationists. America-Firsters. Liberty Leaguers, And, unless I'm entirely mistaken, some officers of the German-American Bund."

"Look here," said Stan. "Robert Strecker. He was an officer of the Bund and America-First, too. What kind of man have we had working in the White House?"

"A bold man," said Kennelly. "Bold enough to leave an address book like this in an unlocked desk."

"Ha!" said Stan. "Here's Julie. A local telephone number. Just 'Julie.' "

"I don't think he meant ever to return to this office," said Mrs. Roosevelt. "I have a sense that he expected to be killed doing whatever it was he was out to do."

"Why would you think that?" asked Stan.

"He was obviously an obsessive pipe smoker," she said. "Four pipes on his desk. But there was no pipe on his person, was there, Ed?"

"No."

"I should guess he planned his days so he was never

without a pipe. Leaving here with a pistol in his pocket but no pipe . . . Well, it suggests to me, perhaps fancifully, that he meant to do something desperate and did not expect to survive."

Ed smiled. "It extends logic a bit, but I wouldn't be surprised if you're right."

"I would like to know," said Stan, "just how he got from here to the Lincoln Bedroom."

"This may have helped," said Kennelly. He had taken Weyrich's wallet from his pocket and carried it in a manila envelope. From it he extracted an identification card—

EXECUTIVE OFFICE OF THE PRESIDENT
IDENTITY CARD

NAME: Paul S. Weyrich
AGE:34 SEX:M HT:5'8" WT:173
EYES:Bl HAIR:Brn
Special Counsel to the President,
Diplomatic Affairs

ISSUED: 11/21/42 ✪

Kennelly was right about the identity card. They went to two security desks between Weyrich's office and the main corridor of the White house—at the exit from the West Wing and the entrance to the White House itself. At each one they heard the same story—

"Oh, sure. Mr. Weyrich had full clearance. That's what the star means. He was working on some kind of papers that the President needed in the conference that's going on. He was carrying a green leather folder stamped with the Presidential seal in gold. He said he was supposed to deliver that to the Diplomatic Reception Room."

"Did anyone else pass through from the West Wing into the White House this evening?" asked Mrs. Roosevelt.

"Well . . . Julie Finch, Mr. Weyrich's secretary. She was with Mr. Weyrich. She had clearance to enter the mansion and sometimes came in, carrying papers for the President or for Mr. Hopkins. She checked out again about half an hour later. Mr. Weyrich did not check out at all. Uh . . . we've heard what happened to him."

"Nothing is secret here," said Stan wryly.

Mrs. Roosevelt frowned and shook her head. "Where is the green leather folder and the papers that were in it? Was he carrying a pistol because he was authorized to carry one, to guard secret documents?"

"No," said Stan. "*I* am not authorized to carry a gun in the White House. Ed's was taken from him at the gate. Nobody but uniformed White House policemen and uniformed military personnel can carry firearms on the grounds or in the buildings."

"Which returns us to the question: How did *he* get his gun in here?" said Kennelly.

"Far more important," said Mrs. Roosevelt, "*why* was he carrying a gun in the White House?"

III

THOUGH SHE HAD NOT retired until nearly 2:00 A.M., Mrs. Roosevelt rose early. She phoned downstairs for a breakfast tray and asked if the President's breakfast had been ordered and delivered. The kitchen said no, and she asked to be called when his breakfast *was* brought up.

While waiting for her tray to come, she sat with Malvina "Tommy" Thompson, her secretary, and dictated two "My Day" columns. She took notice of the tenth anniversary of Hitler's notorious order for the burning of books. "If he thought to suppress books by burning them," she wrote, "he was badly frustrated because the burning only served to increase peoples' interest in them, even in Germany, and the authors were read more than ever."

Thomas Mann, for example, was more highly regarded in Germany after his books were burned than he had been before. *Buddenbrooks* was one of her favorite novels. And he was only one. "Ideas cannot be burned," she wrote. "If you want to destroy an idea, you must do it by *persuading* people that it is invalid. Brute force persuades no one."

Her daughter and her grandchildren were visiting and occupied the guest suite directly across the hall from her own rooms and the President's. She stepped across to say good morning to Anna only to discover that she had taken the children out to play on the lawn

The President did not sleep late, though the Prime Minister would, and the conference would not reconvene much before noon. Mrs. Roosevelt got the ring from the kitchen and went to the President's room.

He was sitting up in bed as always, with his breakfast tray across his lap and newspapers spread out around him. Fala was scampering around, wagging his tail, and shamelessly begging for the bites he knew his master would offer him. The President always ate a full breakfast—bacon or sausage with eggs and toast, juice, and coffee. Fala would eat his share of the toast, as morsels offered from the President's hand.

Mrs. Roosevelt did not sit down. "I shall take only a moment of your time," she said. "I mean not to trouble you with anything during the conference."

"But you've come to tell me about the death of Weyrich. I was told about him last night and was certain you'd be about your duties as the Sherlock Holmes of the White House."

"I need to ask a few questions."

"Shoot. Sit down, Babs. Sit down."

"No. I shall only be a moment, Franklin. Tell me briefly: Who was Paul Weyrich and why was he working for you?"

"He was a Chicago lawyer, a specialist in international law. Fine credentials. I had him working on a number of projects, chiefly planning the international organization I hope to see formed after the war. Organizing a thing like that and getting nations to adhere to it—not to mention getting the treaty through the Senate—presents unbelievable complexities. Weyrich knew the difficulties and had specific ideas about how to meet most of them. I thought I was lucky to have him."

"Did you know he was involved with the Liberty League, America-first, Father Coughlin, Colonel McCormick, and the like?"

"Involved . . . how?"

"Their names were in his address book."

"Maybe it was his enemies list."

"Did you summon him to the conference room last night, to bring some papers?"

The President shook his head. "No."

"Did you summon his secretary to bring anything?"

"No."

"Very well. I'll try not to trouble you further with this matter."

"Babs . . . Winston must not know, if there is any way we can prevent it."

"I understand fully."

• • •

From the President's bedroom Mrs. Roosevelt went directly to the West Wing and to the second-floor office where she had been the night before. The office was closed and locked, though the officer on duty offered to open it if she wanted in.

She turned to the tiny room next door. A tearful young woman sat there, typing on an Underwood typewriter.

"Miss Finch?"

"I'm Julie . . . *Mrs. Roosevelt!*"

Julie Finch was a blond. Her eyebrows and lashes were blond. Even so, her hair had been treated with something to give it an unnatural golden-yellow color. Otherwise, the First Lady's impression of Julie was that she was extraordinarily beautiful. Her face was pretty—soft but not fat-soft—with a pert nose and great blue eyes. She was wearing a knee-length black skirt and a white blouse, with a little golden cross hanging on a delicate gold chain around her neck.

Her eyes were dimmed with tears. They glistened on her cheeks.

"Did you just now learn what happened?" Mrs. Roosevelt asked sympathetically.

"Yes," Julie sobbed. "No one thought to call *me* last night."

"Could anyone have reached you?"

"Of course. Paul called me at home all the time. Besides bein' in his address book, my phone number is in my personal file." She spoke with a faintly Southern accent.

"But, my dear, why *should* anyone have called you? So far as anyone knew, you were just his secretary. *I* know you were in love with him, but—"

Shock registered on Julie's face. "How do you know that?"

"We searched his office last night and found a letter you wrote him."

Julie covered her face with her hands and sobbed. Then abruptly she stiffened. "I can't even offer you a chair in this squalid little office," she said bitterly.

"Let us go to *my* office," said Mrs. Roosevelt. "I must tell you that an agent of the Secret Service and a detective with the DC police want to ask you some questions. We can meet them more comfortably in my study."

"Before we go, let me show you letters *he* wrote to *me*."

She opened her desk drawer and pulled out four typewritten notes. The first one read—

> Dear J^{u}lie,
> Wo^{u}ld yo^{u} pay me the ~~honnor~~ honor of allowing me to take yo^{u} to dinner this evening? If not this evening, then tomorrow evening? Please say yes.
>
> Paul

Then—

My very darling Julie,
A word of thank~~e~~s for last night. Not of~~f~~ten in his whole life does a man meet a girl so loving and ~~carrying~~ caring. You are truly my ~~Valantine~~ Valentine.

Paul

The third letter said—

Honey Baby,
You are tru~~yl~~ly a miracle! I didn't know I could be so happy!

The fourth message struck a note of caution—

Dearest,
Being with you is true ~~hevven~~ heaven. We have got to do some thinking just the same. I'm not sure what would happen to us if it got around that we ~~meean~~ mean so much to each other. I hope you haven't spoken to anybody about us. Don't forget that if I lost my job here I would probably be drafted, and we don't either one of us want that. I'll see you tonight, but <u>be carefull!</u>

"Why did Mr. Weyrich communicate by typewritten

notes when his office was next to yours? He must have seen you every day."

"Paul was a shy man, basically. When he tried to talk about anything that involved his emotions, he stuttered. So far as typin' his notes is concerned, try to read a sample of his handwriting. Look at his signature. I had a lot more notes from him. I kept these. I guess you can see why."

"Let us walk over to my study," said Mrs. Roosevelt.

As they walked into the White House from the West Wing, Mrs. Roosevelt and Julie Finch met General Eisenhower, Sarah Churchill, and Kay Summersby. The general's face beamed with his trademark grin, and he extended his hand to the First Lady.

"You know Sarah, of course," he said. "And you met Kay Summersby last evening."

Mrs. Roosevelt introduced Julie—"Secretary to one of the President's advisers."

"I'm showing the ladies around the White House," said the general. "We've done the state rooms. I was hoping we could pick up coffee in the kitchen."

"You will be more comfortable if you have it brought up," said Mrs. Roosevelt. "Use the Private Dining Room. You know where it is—opposite the State Dining Room."

General Eisenhower was conspicuously enjoying leading the two attractive young women through the mansion. Kay was obviously impressed and grateful.

"You have seen far grander houses," Mrs. Roosevelt said to Sarah. "Buckingham Palace . . . Blenheim Palace . . ."

"None where such power was concentrated," said Sarah.

"It's a lovely house," said Kay. "It's grand and beautiful without overwhelming one. Some of the English stately homes are far bigger than any conceivable useful purpose could justify."

"Enjoy your visit," said Mrs. Roosevelt. "I know I will see you again during your stay."

On the second floor, Kennelly and Szczygiel were waiting in the First Lady's study. The coffee and pastries she had already ordered were waiting, and the four sat down and took cups and plates.

"Miss Finch," said Stan, "you and Mr. Weyrich entered the White House last night. You left after about half an hour. He never did. Why were you here? What was the purpose of your visit?"

"The President called him and asked him to come to the conference room and bring some papers. He asked me to come along with my shorthand pad, in case the President wanted to dictate anything." As an element of her accent, Julie said "Presi-*dent*."

"I am afraid that can't be true," said Mrs. Roosevelt. "I spoke to the President this morning, and he told me he did not summon Mr. Weyrich to the conference room."

"I can't help that. It's what Paul told me."

"Did he go to the conference room? Did he enter it?"

"He went in the Map Room. He told me to wait outside. After just a minute or so, he came out. He'd been carrying a green leather folder, and when he came out he didn't have it."

Stan got up and left the room.

"In police work we have to be sneaky, Miss Finch," said Ed Kennelly. "Mr. Szczygiel and I searched your office last night." He smiled at Mrs. Roosevelt. "After you went to bed, ma'am." He turned again to Julie. "You are in possession of some letters, apparently from Weyrich, suggesting that he was having a love affair with you. A letter from you, found in *his* desk, is far more suggestive. In your letter, you mention a tie clasp. Would that be *this* tie clasp?"

Ed produced from his pocket a necktie clasp bearing symbols of the Masonic Lodge. He put it in front of her, beside her coffee cup.

Julie sobbed. "Yes! Yes! I gave it to him. Where did you get it?"

"The medical examiner found it in his left-hand pants pocket, with his keys. He wasn't wearing it."

"It wasn't good enough for him to be seen wearing. It was too cheap. He carried it. He showed it to me, showed me that he carried it all the time, that it was important to him. *I* was important to him. But I was like the tie clasp: too common. It was all very fine to— Well, you know what. But he didn't want to be *seen* with me. I was too cheap a woman to be identified with Paul Weyrich."

"Miss Finch . . ." the First Lady said quietly, "Mr. Weyrich was carrying a loaded pistol. Have you any idea why?"

"*No!* My God, no!"

"Did you ever see the pistol?"

Julie hyperventilated. "If you found a gun on him . . . when he was dead . . . it was *planted* on him. He wouldn't have known how to use a pistol! Comin' from where *I* do, I know how to shoot a pistol or a rifle or a shotgun; but Paul was a city boy."

"They are not unacquainted with guns in Chicago," said Mrs. Roosevelt dryly.

"I assume you were in love with him," said Kennelly.

She ran her hands down her face. She nodded. "Absolutely. Paul didn't know this . . . but . . . I may be carrying his baby."

"*Are* you pregnant?" Ed asked. "Are you carrying anybody's baby?"

"I'm . . . not sure. But if I am, it's his. It couldn't be anybody else's. I'm not the kind of girl who . . . well, you know what I mean. If I'm carrying a baby, it is Paul's."

Finally Stanlislaw Szczygiel returned. He poured fresh coffee into his cup to warm it up and then sat down. "I'm afraid there's a small discrepancy in your story, Miss Finch," he said. "We keep very tight security on the Situation Room, or Map Room as it's more often called. Duty there is shared by a senior agent and by an officer of the army or navy. They keep a log of every entrance to the room. Weyrich did not enter that room last night."

Mrs. Roosevelt frowned. "If you've told an untruth, Miss Finch, correct it now. Lying in the investigation of a murder is a very bad thing to do."

"Am I a suspect?"

"You might be. Depending."

The young woman wiped her eyes with two fingers and glanced at the First Lady, Ed, and Stan. "I didn't want to say why I was in the White House. It's embarrassing."

"Embarrassing or not, you had better tell us why," said Kennelly sternly.

"Paul thought it would be a great adventure if we . . . If we . . . You know what, in one of the state rooms of the White House."

"And did you?"

"Yes."

"Where?"

"In the Red Room. On the floor. In the dark. We used two cushions but didn't sit on any of the furniture. Paul thought it was a great romantic adventure. I thought it was risky."

"What time did you leave the Red Room?" asked Mrs. Roosevelt.

"I don't know what time it was. I don't wear a watch."

"Where did you go and what did you do?"

"I went out through the West Wing and through the White House grounds to look for a cab. Paul gave me money for a cab, as he usually did when I worked late or was with him late. I caught a cab, finally, and went home."

"Where did he go?"

"I don't know. I left him in the Red Room." She sobbed. "I never saw him again."

IV

"I DON'T BELIEVE HER," said Kennelly when Julie had left them.

"Nor do I," said Szczygiel.

"Well . . . I am not inclined to believe all she says. But not believing her solves nothing," said Mrs. Roosevelt. "Mr. Weyrich entered the White House carrying a gun. Let us suppose that Miss Finch somehow got behind him and struck him a fatal blow. Let us suppose she did it because she resented the cavalier way she was being treated by a man she loved. That does not explain the gun. It does not explain why Mr. Weyrich was in the Lincoln Bedroom. It does not explain how he got there."

"They did not do what she said in the Red Room," said Kennelly.

"They did not do it at all, I suspect," said Szczygiel.

"Why do you think that?" asked Mrs. Roosevelt.

Both men shrugged.

"I suspect they did," said the First Lady. "Miss Finch

impresses me as a cheeky young woman, apt to engage in such conduct—and also a naive person, apt to be taken advantage of."

"Which leads us to . . . ?" asked Ed.

"To nothing much," said Mrs. Roosevelt. "Some work lies ahead of us."

Even so important a conference as Trident had to be interrupted for a few minutes to allow the President to meet briefly and be photographed with personalities who were contributing to the war effort by their appearances at War Bond rallies and going on USO tours.

One of the entertainers who had given much of himself was a young man called Danny Kaye. Mrs. Roosevelt had to confess that she did not know the name. Since he was going to appear at the White House to receive the thanks of the President, and since she would be responsible for talking to him after a very brief moment with the President, the First Lady asked for and received films of his performances. She found him puzzling but immensely amusing. Hyperactive almost to the point of hysteria, he was irresistible.

He was not much different in person from how he appeared on stage. The broad, innocent smile that characterized him could not, apparently, be suppressed. He was simply a natural performer who loved to entertain.

He was accompanied by his wife, Sylvia Fine, who was his composer and manager and—as Mrs. Roosevelt suspected—his calmer-downer, the woman who made his life possible.

After they left the President in the Oval Office, she took the couple to the Private Dining Room for lunch. They were joined there by Sarah Churchill, who was an admirer of Danny Kaye.

"Oh, Mr. Kaye," said Sarah, "I wish you would do your recitation of Russian composers."

It was as though Kaye had been gunpowder waiting to be ignited. His face lit up in a broad grin, his blue eyes bulged, and he struck a comic pose. "*Rimsky*—!" he exclaimed, almost yelled. Then in phenomenally rapid-fire speech, clearly enunciating every syllable—"Korsakov-Rachmaninoff-Prokofiev-Tchaikovsky-Stravinsky-Moussorgsky-Glinka-Balakirev-Borodin-Khatchaturian . . . *AND . . . Dmitri Shostakovich*!" Without so much as pausing for breath, he went through it backward—"Shostakovich-Khatchaturian-Borodin-Balakirev-Glinka-Moussorgsky-Stravinsky-Tchaikovsky-Prokofiev-Rachmaninoff . . . *AND . . . Nicolai Andreyevich Rrrrimsky-Korsakov!*"

Mrs. Roosevelt laughed. "Wonderful, Mr. Kaye!"

Kaye turned up his hands and shrugged. "It could be better," he said, "if the Russians had more composers."

While the First Lady was meeting Danny Kaye and Sylvia Fine, Ed Kennelly and Stan Szczygiel drove to Paul Weyrich's apartment to execute a search warrant. They ate sandwiches and drank coffee in the car on the way.

The man had lived well. The apartment had not been rented furnished, and the furniture that Weyrich had purchased was posh, as were the rugs and drapes. There was just one bedroom, but the great four-poster bed was an antique that had probably originated in an antebellum plantation house in Virginia or Maryland. A massive mahogany bureau matched it. The centerpiece of the living room was a long Victorian cherry settee upholstered in black horsehair. The wood was elegantly carved, as was the wood of two side chairs that did not match the settee but were in the same style.

A small bookcase was filled with books. Most of them were novels by such writers as Ernest Hemingway, James M. Cain, Willa Cather, and Zelda Fitzgerald. He noticed, though, that one book was a political tract by Elizabeth Dilling, titled *The Roosevelt Red Record and Its Background: A Handbook for Patriots*. Kennelly was familiar with it. It had been published almost ten years ago and had at one time been seen in many people's homes. It was, essentially, a list of people and organizations that Mrs. Dilling claimed were involved in a worldwide Communist conspiracy. Among the people listed, Mrs. Roosevelt was prominent. So were Felix Frankfurter, H. L. Mencken, Chiang Kai-shek, and Mahatma Gandhi. The cover art suggested that President Roosevelt was to be compared to Marx, Lenin, and Stalin.

A yellowed old pamphlet had been stuck in the pages as a bookmark. Published by an organization called the Silver Shirts, it was a heavy-handed, clumsy anti-Semitic tract. Among the prominent "Jews" that it condemned was "Franklin D. Rosenfeldt" and "Alfred E. Schmidt."

One end of the living room was a dining alcove, furnished with a solid pedestal table and four chairs.

Paintings hung on the walls—genre paintings of English racehorses, melons and pewter, and braces of birds killed by hunters. Other frames held splendid black-and-white photographs of Washington scenes. One picture was a nude, photographed from behind. A slender young woman, standing on her toes, parted a pair of curtains just enough to allow her to look out and to allow the sunshine to light her body, leaving her back in shadow. The picture was, beyond question, a minor work of art: sensitively done, without the slightest suggestion of eroticism in the nude body.

Weyrich's collection of pipes and tobacco was prominent, on this table and that, also on a windowsill. He had meerschaums and a calabash, even a hookah.

The kitchen was equipped with a white-enamel gas range with lids that folded down to hide the burners when they were not in use, also a big Coldspot refrigerator. There was a kitchen table, but it was not used for eating or to prepare food; an Omega photographic enlarger and three enamel trays for chemicals stood in a row across the tabletop. The kitchen cabinets were half-filled with photo chemicals and boxes of paper.

"Wonder what he photographed," said Stan. "I mean—"

"Could he have been a spy?" Ed finished the thought.

The question was probably answered when they

returned to the living room and looked at the P W initials on the framed photographs. Two of the pictures were of a winter snowfall in Washington, others of the cherry trees in blossom. Though the photos were all in black and white, Weyrich had captured the beauty of the blossoms on the trees and reflected in water. The nude was entirely chaste, artistically posed and photographed.

A framed photograph sitting on the night table beside his bed answered the question more fully, and another question besides. It was a picture of Julie Finch in her underwear, sitting on the horsehair couch in the living room. Her expression showed embarrassment, even humiliation—together with grim determination to sit for this picture and get it over with.

The camera was in the bedroom: a Rolleiflex, an expensive German camera, equipped with a Kalart flash gun. It was no spy camera. To take pictures, the photographer held it against his chest and stared down at the image on horizontal ground glass. Its optics were the envy of the world. A photographer who owned a Rolleiflex was recognized as owning one of the finest cameras made.

A small album in a drawer of the night table contained pictures of Julie in white panties and brassiere and stockings held up by a garter belt.

A box in the bureau contained other photographs of two young women, nude. The photos were perhaps another advantage of owning a Rolleiflex. The photographer had to be recognized as serious, not a snapshot shooter. Many a young woman who would not have done it otherwise, relented and undressed, partially or altogether, when she faced a Rolleiflex. Most of the pictures had pretensions at least to being art; only the pictures of Julie were in a pinup style. By her apparent modesty, her refusal to pose nude, she had inadvertently produced pictures distinctly more sensual than the nudes.

In the top drawer of the bureau they found a box of .32-caliber cartridges. "Which suggests," said Stan, "that the gun you found on him was his, not one shoved into his jacket after he was dead."

They continued their search. After a time Ed asked, "Does it occur to you that something is missing here?"

"Such as?"

"Well . . . Weyrich came here from Chicago. It was still his home, and we know he went back from time to time. How can it be, then, that there is no luggage in his apartment? No suitcase. No valise. Mrs. Roosevelt suggested he did not mean to go back to his office after he did whatever he meant to do in the Lincoln Bedroom. I wonder if he meant to come back here, either. I wonder if he were not packed and had not stashed his luggage somewhere."

"Speculation . . ." said Stan.

"Sometimes speculation leads to the truth."

They went on to Julie Finch's boardinghouse to execute another search warrant.

"It ain't reg'lar," complained a woman who introduced herself as Mrs. Bogardus and said she was owner of the house. "It ain't becuz another girl lives in that room, too, and you'll be searchin' through *her* things, too. How you gonna know what's one girl's and what's th' other's?"

"Why don't you come and watch?" Kennelly suggested.

"I'll do it." As they climbed the broad front stairs of the Victorian house, the heavy Mrs. Bogardus puffed. But she said, "What I get is Guv'mint Girls. Used to be, I rented one room, one girl, strictly. But in these times they double up and worse. Puts an awful strain on the bathrooms."

The room that Julie shared was on the front of the house, was bright and cheery, and featured a cushioned window seat. It was furnished with one heavy oak double bed; the two young women slept together, which was not unusual for Government Girls in 1943. It had a Victorian settee upholstered with black horsehair, a sturdy pedestal table, and two antique straight chairs upholstered in maroon plush. There was one chest of drawers with a mirror mounted on top. The tenants had supplemented it with two foot lockers.

"You rent only to females, Mrs. Bogardus?" Szczygiel asked.

"You bet. Uh-huh! Otherwise I'd have to stay up all night patrollin' th' halls."

"Well . . . we have to go through the personal things. Sit down. We won't take long."

The bureau drawers were filled with nothing but what the two men expected: women's clothes. No gun. No ammunition. Nothing incriminating or suspicious. The closet was jammed with two women's clothes.

The foot lockers were locked, but the keys were in the top drawer of the bureau. Kennelly unlocked one.

"I think that'n is Eva's," said Mrs. Bogardus.

"Eva . . . ?"

"Lee."

The foot lockers were obviously for personal things. Eva Lee had an old Bible in hers, with two or three other books. The Bible was stuffed with letters. Kennelly flipped through them, but none was from Weyrich. Under a towel he found a half-empty fifth of bourbon: Old Granddad. Because having liquor in their rooms likely violated one of the rules of the boardinghouse, Kennelly covered it before Mrs. Bogardus could see it.

In Julie's locker Kennelly found a bundle of letters from Weyrich. He scanned each of them. They were love letters. Better said, they were erotic letters. One read—

> I have to confess. You did not lose your *you-know-whats.* I stuffed them in my overcoat pocket. They are under my pillow and when I am alone I am not ~~quiet~~ quite alone. You are there sort of. The delicious smell of you is on them. I mean your Cologne water but more than that I mean your *natural* smell. In the night I pull the you-know-whats up tp my face and sniff. Well, it's better than not having you there at all.

It was evidence of nothing much, except that it told something of the personality of Paul Weyrich—including a certain recklessness. The rest of the letters were similar.

Another bundle of letters was from another man, named Tim. He, too, typed his letters—

> Please do not say to me that you doubt my love. It is real and undying. Only circumstances prevent my devoting myself entirely to you.
>
> Enclosed is $10. Please see a doctor immediately and find out if you are carrying a baby. And let me know.
>
> All my love. All.

In a corner of the locker lay a Kodak, a folding camera, together with a dozen or more envelopes of snapshots and negatives. Kennelly did not want to look through a hundred or more snapshots, especially when he saw that nearly all of them were trivial: people holding silly poses and grinning. Some of the pictures were of Weyrich. When he had been aiming his Rolleiflex at scenery, Julie had been aiming her Kodak at him.

Several snapshots were of Julie. She was standing somewhere in front of a tree, mugging. In one picture another young woman stood beside her.

Kennelly handed that picture to Mrs. Bogardus. "Is that by any chance Miss Lee, standing there with Miss Finch?"

"Sure," said the landlady. "That's Eva."

When she handed the snapshot back to Kennelly, he handed it to Szczygiel. The Secret Service agent studied it, then nodded almost imperceptibly at Kennelly.

The two men glanced around the room a little more, then thanked Mrs. Bogardus and left.

"Does it mean anything or not mean anything?" Szczygiel asked as they drove away.

"Well, it's suggestive," said Kennelly. "Julie could have gotten very upset over that."

He referred to the fact that the young woman Mrs. Bogardus identified in the snapshot as Eva Lee was one of the models Weyrich had photographed nude.

They reported to Mrs. Roosevelt.

"I have been reviewing Mr. Weyrich's personnel file," she said. "Also Miss Finch's. Mr. Weyrich had a rather spectacular career. He was a graduate of the University of Michigan. He was only thirty-four, but he had attained prominence as a lawyer specializing in international law, chiefly in matters involving international trade, and was earning a substantial amount of money. He took the job here in September of 1940. I am not quite sure why."

"I can answer that," said Stan. "As a member of the President's advisory staff, he was exempt from the draft."

"I hope you are not being cynical, but I suspect you are right. The President used Mr. Weyrich's expertise in such matters as the lend-lease agreements, the transfer of the overage destroyers to Britain, the seizure of French ships—including the *Normandie*—in American ports, and so on. Above all, he was working on a draft of a great treaty establishing a new international organization to replace the old League of Nations. He never married. He had something of a reputation in the Midwest as an accomplished amateur photographer, who won ribbons in a great many shows. Among those who sent letters recommending him—surprisingly, I should think—was Wendell Willkie."

"Did he leave a family?" asked Ed Kennelly.

"Both parents and two brothers," said Mrs. Roosevelt sadly. "His father has worked for the Chicago *Tribune* for thirty years and is said to be a personal friend of Colonel McCormick. His elder brother works for the paper, too."

"Bertie McCormick," Stan sneered. "A professional Roosevelt-hater."

"Colonel McCormick has more money than good sense," said the First Lady primly.

"He seems to have been a loner in the White House," said Stan. "Apart from his secretary, he seems not to have made any special friends."

"Miss Finch's file is not without interest," said Mrs. Roosevelt. "In the first place, her name is not really Miss Julie Finch; it is Mrs. Lawrence Mellon, Jr. She was married at age seventeen and divorced at twenty. She is the mother of a child being reared by her mother-in-law. A daughter. She is no ordinary civil-service employee or

Government Girl. Her father-in-law is a member of Congress from Tennessee and asked Harry Hopkins to get her a job in Washington, to get her away from Tennessee, where she is an embarrassment to the Mellons. Congressman Mellon has been an important supporter of the President's legislative programs, and Harry was glad to do him a favor."

"How was she an embarrassment to the Mellons?" asked Ed.

"*In their judgment,* she fell in love too easily and too easily surrendered her favors. I suspect that rural Tennessee judges such things rather narrowly as compared to how we might judge them here."

"Well, she didn't take long to fall in love with Weyrich and surrender her favors," Ed remarked.

"Changing the subject," said Mrs. Roosevelt, "what would you judge was the murder weapon?"

"The proverbial blunt object," said Kennelly. "The wound was too large to be made by just a blackjack. It was made by something bigger and heavier, like a sash weight."

"Whatever it was, it is missing, is it not?"

Ed nodded. "It is missing. The killer carried it away."

"In your judgment, could Miss Finch have wielded such a weapon with sufficient force to crush a man's skull and cause his death?"

"Yes. But she would have to get behind him. And she would have had to be *carrying* the weapon. I have to wonder if she wasn't standing in front of him, holding his attention while someone else struck him from behind."

"That would mean that *three people* were in the Lincoln Bedroom, that three got past the guards working the second floor halls. Tell me, Mr. Szczygiel, just what was the extent of Officer Willoughby's duty area?"

"The East Hall, the ramp to the Stair Hall, and the Stair Hall. The main, formal stairs, called Stairs Number One or the East Stairs were assigned to him, and he would go partway down as he made rounds, to make sure no one was hiding on the stairs. Beyond that the West Sitting Hall was his responsibility. Half way along the West Sitting Hall he would meet the man guarding the door to the President's bedroom. He probably would have a word with that man, then work his way back."

The First Lady nodded. "When the President sits in the West Sitting Hall, he can see all the way to the East Hall. He could see someone entering the Lincoln Bedroom. The entire length of the second floor halls were in sight to a man patrolling those halls."

"Except when he went into the North Hall for a moment, which he probably did, and—more important—when he went down the East Stairs," said Stan.

"I don't see," said Kennelly, "how anyone could have sneaked up from downstairs and into the Lincoln Bedroom."

"Well, someone did," said Stan.

"There is a way," said Mrs. Roosevelt. "Suppose those

in the Lincoln Bedroom had not come up from the first floor but down from the third floor?"

"How could they do that?" Ed asked.

"Rather simply, actually," she said. "One could start from the ground floor or the first floor. One could use either of the two elevators. On the first and second floors, the elevators do not open directly on the main halls but on elevator lobbies. Men on guard in the main halls would not see the elevator go by on its way to the third floor. If they noticed the elevator going up, they probably would take no particular notice; people live in the third-floor rooms. What is more, the secondary stairway, what is called Stairs Number Two, go up through hallways separated from the main halls. A person climbing those stairs might well pass through the first and second floors unnoticed. Now—

"A separate narrow set of stairs comes down from the third floor to the second and ends in a small stair lobby just across the East Hall from the Lincoln Bedroom. A careful person, listening and peeking out from the stair lobby, could watch for Officer Willoughby. When he went down the East Stairs, that person could easily cross the East Hall and enter the Lincoln Bedroom."

"In sight of the agent guarding the door to the President's bedroom," said Kennelly skeptically.

"That man's focus is on the private living quarters in the west end of the building," said Stan.

"Besides which," added Mrs. Roosevelt, "with Mr. Churchill and his staff using the Queen's Bedroom Suite, the man might well assume anyone moving in the East Hall was British. No, I think reaching the Lincoln Bedroom last night would not have presented insuperable difficulty."

"Assuming," said Stan, "that someone knew the White House and its current routines very, very well."

Mrs. Roosevelt met for dinner that evening with an ad hoc committee of women representing the Women's Christian Temperance Union, the Wesleyan Society, Daughters of the American Revolution, and other groups. The subject was the morals of young women working in Washington. The First Lady suggested that decent living quarters was the worst problem and suggested that some of these women might be able to take a girl or two into their homes as boarders, which would enable them to guide and supervise. She sensed that the suggestion did not generate much enthusiasm.

She overheard a woman say, "Well, that's what we had to expect from *that* source. A Government Girl living in *my* house. I hardly think so."

"How many live in the White House?" another woman asked. "How many live at Hyde Park?"

"Well . . . Hyde Park is some distance from Washington."

"Very well. How many English refugee children live at Hyde Park. These New Deal types can always think of wonderful ways for *other people* to make sacrifices."

V

MRS. ROOSEVELT HAD A sense that Sarah Churchill and Kay Summersby were being left alone in their third-floor rooms while the Prime Minister and General Eisenhower were involved in the long hours of the Trident Conference. Though her own hours were filled to capacity, she felt an obligation to do something to relieve what had to be their boredom. She arranged for them to accompany her on a tour of the city on Thursday morning.

She wore a crepe dress in light violet and white, with a yellow straw hat that had a veil she tucked up so that it covered only a little of her forehead and not her eyes.

Churchill's and Eisenhower's presence in Washington was a deep secret and a matter of national security, so she asked for a White House car that bore no special plates or markings and was used for confidential travel. She would have liked to drive herself, but she was too often recognized behind the wheel when she stopped for a light; and so she sat in the middle of the rear seat with the two young women to her right and left, while an agent of the Secret Service drove. Another anonymous car followed, carrying heavily armed agents.

She could not take these two women inside any of the buildings she pointed out to them, not even inside the Lincoln Memorial. Driving by the Capitol and the Library of Congress, she could only describe what they contained. Interested as they were in the British Embassy, the car could not even slow down, lest someone see one of them and recognize Mrs. Roosevelt.

"Abraham Lincoln," said Sarah. "Surely he represents the best your nation has ever had to offer."

"We think of him constantly in these days," said Mrs. Roosevelt. "He could look out the windows of the White House and see the Confederate army encamped on the Virginia hills. He was the last of our Presidents ever to face the possibility of having to flee Washington in the face of invasion."

"Lovely city, Washington," said Kay. "I should dearly like to live here someday."

"Perhaps you shall," said Mrs. Roosevelt.

"There is no certainty left in the world," said Kay. "Four years ago I believed I knew my future. I was going to be a small-time actress with hopes of becoming something better, and I was going to marry. Then came the war. My fiancé was killed. Acting career . . . pfftt. I'm fortunate I was assigned to drive Ike. Don't know I'd have ever seen Washington, otherwise."

"General Eisenhower holds Kay in very high regard," said Sarah. "He trusts her with everything."

"Well . . . not everything," said Kay.

"In London she is regarded not just as his driver but as one of his more trusted advisers."

"Ike," said Kay, "likes to unburden himself at the end of a day. It's his way of reviewing and organizing his thoughts. He needs to relax, too, so we try to find two more for a rubber of bridge."

"I have known General Eisenhower since he was a major and an aide to General MacArthur," said Mrs. Roosevelt. "He has risen in this world, owing I am sure to his abilities."

"He will rise once more," said Kay. "When General Marshall comes to England to take command of the forces that will invade France, Ike will be appointed Army Chief of Staff. When that happens, I may have the opportunity to live in Washington after all."

"One complication stands in the way," said Sarah. "General Sir Alan Brooke wants that command, and as Chief of the Imperial General Staff he has a heavy claim on it."

"Montgomery wants it too," said Kay, allowing a note of distaste to creep into her voice.

"Well, that's why they are having the Trident Conference," said Mrs. Roosevelt. "To decide questions like that."

"Ike doesn't think it will be decided before the end of the year," said Kay.

"I assume he very much wants to command the invasion," said Mrs. Roosevelt.

"Yes, but General Marshall is his mentor and his longtime good friend. Ike doesn't want to take from Marshall what Marshall deserves. And wants."

Ed Kennelly had spent many years investigating crimes. He had learned things. He had learned that when a traveler rents a locker in a railroad station and fails to return for the contents by the end of the rental period—normally twenty-four hours—the locker company empties the locker and holds the contents in a room. Having seen no luggage in Weyrich's apartment, he wondered if Weyrich might have put his luggage in a locker, in anticipation of a quick departure from Washington.

"I can get a warrant," he said to the officious shirtsleeved clerk who had told him that even a DC police detective could not gain access to that special room, much less open any luggage. "I can also rack your ass into trouble. I'm investigating a murder."

The man turned down the corners of his mouth in an expression of deep displeasure—so much that he wrinkled his whole chin. "Well . . . this sort of thing is most irregular."

"Murder tends to be irregular," said Kennelly.

They entered the heavily locked room, where luggage and a wide variety of other things were scattered on the floor and on shelves. "When would this locker have been rented?" the clerk asked.

"It may not have been rented at all," said Kennelly. "We didn't find a locker key on the body. But we didn't find luggage where luggage should have been. He would have rented it Monday or Tuesday."

"If Tuesday, the contents of the locker would still be in it. The rental is for twenty-four hours, but we don't open lockers on the day following the rental. We allow that much of a grace period."

"Well, what do you have for Monday?"

The clerk pointed out an assortment of luggage assembled in a knot not far from the door.

Ed looked it over, frowning distastefully. "I don't think any of this stuff is what I'm looking for. My murder victim had money and would have had better luggage than any of this. So . . . my friend . . . let's start opening the Tuesday lockers."

"I'll need authority for that."

"You've got authority, the authority of the badge I showed you. Look, fellow, I've done this before. It's no big deal. Let's make it easy on both of us."

The clerk walked along the ranks of coin-operated lockers, checking the times when they had been rented. He found just four that had been rented on Tuesday and were still locked.

"Open," Kennelly said gruffly.

The clerk used a master key. The first locker he opened, rented before noon on Tuesday, contained a handsome leather Gladstone bag. And a nonmatching leather valise. Both bore initials in gold letters: PW.

"Let's take 'em to your office."

"But what if the man comes back?"

"He's *not* comin' back. I can promise you that."

The clerk carried the Gladstone bag, and Ed carried the valise into a cluttered office. Opening first the Gladstone, Ed found suggestive evidence: suits with the labels of Chicago clothiers, monogrammed silk shirts with the label of a Chicago shirtmaker. In the valise: a one-way ticket to Los Angeles in the name of Paul Weyrich, a passport in the same name, and a big manila envelope stuffed with cash. Counted, the cash amounted to $21,500.

Ed summoned uniformed officers from the station and recruited them as witnesses while he wrote out a general inventory of the contents of the luggage and signed it. The inventory was a receipt for what he was taking, and he handed it to the clerk. The two bags went into a marked police car for their trip, first to the White House, then to the property room at headquarters.

Before he could enter the White House carrying the bag and the valise, Kennelly had to allow them to be opened and thoroughly searched by an army lieutenant and a uniformed White House policeman. Both men knew him well; even so they checked his identification as though they had never seen him before. They took his sidearm and locked it in a steel box.

The First Lady met him in her study. She was standing at a window when he came in, staring at the Washington Monument, the cherry blossoms, and in the distance across the Tidal Basin, the new Jefferson Memorial. It was one of the times of year when Washington could be beautiful—which it wasn't in the subtropical heat of summer or the yellow dank of winter. Her straw hat lay on her breakfront.

"I've called for Stan to join us," she told Kennelly. "I . . . Staring at Washington, I sometimes think of the first time I came to live here. We were not very important then, though I think Franklin expected he would be President someday, as Uncle Ted had been. He would have been like Uncle Ted if not—I mean vigorous to the point of being hyperactive. Remember the newsreel of the President chopping down a tree? Franklin would have been like that, though chopping trees would not have been his choice of an exercise. I remember his ice boat. It seemed to me a reckless thing to do, to go skimming over the frozen Hudson on sail-driven runners. He— Well, Ed, I do go on. Have you found the luggage?"

Kennelly was gratified that she called him Ed, but he did not venture to call her Eleanor. "I thought we'd go through it together, ma'am."

"Maybe we should wait for Stan."

They did not have to wait. Szczygiel arrived a moment later.

They placed the two pieces of luggage on the floor, Kennelly and Szczygiel crouched next to them, and they began to examine the contents. The First Lady sat in a chair and watched.

The experienced Ed Kennelly knew what to look for

and where to look for it. Within a minute after opening the Gladstone bag, he had a pair of shoes out on the floor and was prying the heel of one shoe apart with the heaviest blade of his pocketknife. "And so," he grunted. With his fingers he pulled a wad of tissue paper out of the hollow heel of the shoe. Unfolding the paper, he poured four large diamonds on the carpet.

"Mr. Weyrich didn't want to be a poor man if he succeeded in whatever his purpose was and escaped," said the First Lady.

"And we'll find more," said Kennelly. "More, apart from the cash in the valise. Whatever Weyrich was up to, it was to be the final act of his career. He was going out rich, if he could *get* out."

"Let's look at his passport," said Stan.

Paul Weyrich, it appeared, had been a well-traveled man. His visas showed that he had been in Bolivia, Paraguay, and Argentina within the past eighteen months. And since visas were not required to enter Mexico, he may have been there as well.

Packed in the valise was a leather case containing two briar pipes of the highest quality and a quantity of fine, aromatic tobacco.

"What we are looking at contradicts a theory I expressed earlier," said Mrs. Roosevelt. "I suggested he was on a suicide mission, that he had left his pipes in his office because he knew he would have no use for them in the future. Well . . . he would *have* no use for *them* in future. He would use the ones we now see."

"Which means he believed he had an escape route," said Kennelly.

"Through the tightest security ever placed around the White House," said Szczygiel.

Ed kept going through the valise. "Look at this," he said.

He had found a letter—

23/4/43

John,

This introduces you to our trusted friend Weyrich, who has performed a signal service for us. Please accord him the same respect and assistance you would accord me if I had the privilege of being with you.

ROBERT

"Not American to American," said Mrs. Roosevelt.

"You know by—"

"The letter is dated April 23, 1943. An American would abbreviate that '4/23/43.' The writer has abbreviated it '23/4/43,' which is the European practice. It has been the source of some confusion from time to time. A young woman of my acquaintance once arrived in Paris on April 5, 1921 expecting to keep an appointment with a young man who had written that he looked forward to seeing her on '4/5/21.' He had meant the fourth of May. The matter turned out to be to her great good fortune, since she would have been made very unhappy if she had kept the assignation."

"We don't know who 'John' is, and we don't know who 'Robert' is," said Kennelly. "This case gets more and more mysterious."

"The writer, at least, is European," said the First Lady. "Or maybe Latin American."

"Well, let's see what else we've got."

As expected, there were more valuables. Prying open a container of Mum deodorant, Kennelly found no more diamonds but three large square-cut emeralds.

"Alright," said Mrs. Roosevelt. "Not a suicide mission. He expected to get away."

"*And how?*" asked Szczygiel. "And how did he get the gun into the White House?"

"More important than that," said the First Lady, "how did he—to use a strange mode of speech I believe the police use occasionally—how did Mr. Weyrich 'get dead'?"

"And why, on the night when he was trying to carry out his mission, whatever it was, did he have Julie Finch with him?" asked Kennelly. "The young woman is not just an adjunct to this case. She had something important to do with it."

Kennelly poked through the contents of the Gladstone bag. In a moment he began to laugh. "My Lord, here are her 'you-know-whats.' They *were* important to him. He *did* put them under his pillow and was taking them with him to wherever he escaped!"

He lifted a pair of very ordinary white panties.

"How goddamned prosaic can you get?" Kennelly asked. "What kind of man plots something as serious as the assassination of the President of the United States and packs in his luggage a pair of his lover's panties? What kind of guy did we have here?" He sniffed cautiously. "*Worn* panties. She'd had these on!"

"Ed . . ." said Mrs. Roosevelt. "Did you check at the railroad station to see if *she* had a locker?"

"No. I should have. You know . . . I went after Weyrich's locker because there was no luggage in his apartment. Well, there was none in Julie's either. Of course, why should there have been? I—?"

"Just about everyone has a traveling bag, Ed."

"It struck me odd that he had no luggage because I knew he traveled back and forth to Chicago with some regularity. Besides, I figured he was thinking in terms of absquatulating. In her case I . . . just didn't think of it. I should have."

VI

AS THEY CONTINUED TO explore the contents of Weyrich's luggage, the telephone rang. Tommy Thompson answered and reported that Julie Finch was on the line, asking to speak with Mrs. Roosevelt. The First Lady took the call.

"Oh, Mrs. Roosevelt! May I come to see you?"

"I am rather busy at the moment. I suppose I can spare a few minutes if it's important."

"It is *very* important. *Please!*"

"Very well. Come up to the residence and tell the officer on duty to take you to the President's study. I will see you there."

The architecture of the White House affords three large oval rooms on the north facade, stacked on top of one another. The most famous of these oval rooms is the Blue Room on the first floor. Above and below it are oval rooms that are less well-known but have of course the same dimensions. The Trident Conference was meeting in the ground-floor oval room. The oval room on the second floor had long been used as a private office for the President, but to avoid confusion with the Oval Office in the West Wing, it was never called an office but the President's Study. The President worked there sometimes, but it was also the place where he pored over his stamp collection. It was decorated to suit him, with ship models. Knowing the President would not be using the room that afternoon, Mrs. Roosevelt invited Julie to meet with her there.

The girl was tearful. She nearly collapsed into the chair the First Lady offered her.

"What is wrong, my dear?"

Julie sobbed and couldn't speak. She opened her purse and handed Mrs. Roosevelt a letter—

May 10, 1943
Dearest Julie,
By the time you receive this letter I will be a long way from here. By then you will understand why. I will have done something I *have* to do. You will be proud you knew me. For the rest of your life you will be asked what sort of fellow I was.

If anyone gives you any trouble about having had some part in what I did, show them this letter. You had nothing to do with it.

Something different may happen. What I

am going to do may not come out right. Even ~~them~~ then you can use this as proof that you had nothing ~~do we~~ to do with what I did.

If Everything works out OK, it may be possible sometime for me to ask you to come and be with me where I will then be. I hope so.

I am carrying with me a pair of your you-know-whats and will sleep with them under my pillow every night. I guess you know that proves how much I love you. Anyway, it proves how much I will miss you and how much I will want for us to get together again.

Anyway you will always know I love you. You can make something out of that. Like write a book!

Whatever happens, it will be a long time before I see you again. Take good care of yourself.

Paul

The First Lady asked to be allowed to make a photostat of the letter and called in Tommy Thompson to take the letter to the West Wing where photostating equipment was available.

"He said it might not work out okay," Julie wept, nodding emphatically. "Well . . . it didn't."

"The letter is dated Tuesday," said Mrs. Roosevelt. "And you didn't receive it until today? This is Thursday afternoon."

"It came in the morning mail, addressed to me at home. But of course I wasn't *at* home. My roommate wasn't feeling well and left her office at noon. When she found the letter from Paul in the mail, she called me, and I took a cab out and got it."

"Even so, two days . . ."

"He must have put it in the outgoing mail from the West Wing, just before we left the office Tuesday Evening. It would have been late evening before it left the White House, and—Anyway, it didn't reach my boardinghouse until this morning."

"Where is the envelope?" the First Lady asked.

Julie shook her head. "I think I must have left it in the cab."

"Do you believe it?" Kennelly asked Mrs. Roosevelt.

"You mean, believe that she didn't write it herself, to exonerate herself?"

"It arrived two days after it was ostensibly written. A letter mailed Tuesday, even in the evening, should have arrived Wednesday—perhaps in the afternoon delivery. There is no envelope."

"I wonder if it would not be a good idea to interview Eva," said the First Lady.

• • •

Ed Kennelly had seen Winston Churchill briefly during Churchill's 1941 visit, but he had never met him, and he remarked to Mrs. Roosevelt that he would like the opportunity to shake the famous man's hand. She said it could be arranged easily enough if the presidential cocktail hour happened to be in session. In fact, they could not get out of her study except by passing through the cocktail group.

As it happened, the group had assembled around the President in the West Sitting Hall when the First Lady, Kennelly, and Szczygiel came out of her study.

The President presided in his wheelchair where he always did: with his back to the westernmost window of the long second-floor corridor. From there, with no doors closed, he could see all the way to the easternmost window, beside the Lincoln suite. His pince-nez was mounted on his nose, reflecting light, and his signature cigarette holder was atilt in his signature style.

Churchill sat beside him, a snifter of brandy in one hand, a fat cigar in the other, looking something like a butter Buddha that was softening and settling.

Facing the President from the several chairs and couches were the conferees: Prime Minister Winston Churchill, General Sir Alan Brooke, Chief of the Imperial General Staff, General George Marshall, General Dwight Eisenhower, and Admiral Ernest King. Sarah Churchill and Kay Summersby were also there.

"Franklin, I would like to introduce these two gentlemen to your guests. They are Captain Edward Kennelly of the District Police and Agent Stanlislaw Szczygiel of the Secret Service."

"Of course," said the President, and he proceeded to introduce the two men to each of the cocktail-hour guests. "Babs," he said, "is the unofficial Hawkshaw of the White House. After every state dinner we count the spoons, and if we are short she calls in the DC police."

She did not take offense at his so depreciating what she was doing. It was more important that none of these people know about the murder.

"Gentlemen, have a drink with us. I am afraid it will have to be standing, as we seem to be short of chairs."

Kennelly and Szczygiel were elated to be asked to share a drink with this company and tentatively approached the President as he began to pour for them.

But the First Lady cautioned them. "Beware of what he's pouring for you. It has been known to knock people flat." She sat down in a chair vacated for her by Kay Summersby.

The President laughed. "When President Wilson sent troops to Haiti, I was Undersecretary of the Navy and went there to observe. I sampled this rum punch, liked it, and resolved to learn to make it. It consists of rum and orange juice and brown sugar, with a dollop of egg white, all of which we shake vigorously. Perfectly innocent."

"He neglects to tell you he also puts in a teaspoonful of gunpowder," said Mrs. Roosevelt. "Or so it seems, remembering some of the headaches the concoction has caused over the years."

"Like the artillery punch that is so much favored by our regimental messes," said Churchill.

"Maybe I should learn to make that," said President Roosevelt. "What's in it, Winston?"

"Oh, it's a rather complex concoction, and you have to make at least two gallons. You put in a quart of bourbon, a pint of gin, a pint of vodka, I seem to recall, a quart of rum, a bottle of red wine, some grenadine. . . . It must sit for an hour or two to ripen. Then you pour it over a big block of ice that has been frozen from strong black tea. You serve it in cups to which have been added twists of lemon peel."

"Got that, Babs?" the President said ebulliently to Mrs. Roosevelt. "Let's have Mrs. Nesbitt make it for the next state dinner."

"I'm afraid it might be beyond Mrs. Nesbitt's drink-mixing capacities," said Mrs. Roosevelt.

"Making ice water is beyond Henrietta Nesbitt's drink-mixing capacities," said the President, still jovial but with a suggestion of bitterness in his voice. He glanced around at his guests. "Mrs. Nesbitt is a heavy cross I have to bear. She is why the meals served here are so invariably bad."

"I must say, she does seem to have little appreciation of claret," said Churchill.

"Appreciation! Her notion of wine is New York State mucilage," said the President.

"*I* choose the wines served in the White House," said

the First Lady. "Circumstances require me to give some consideration to economy. When the Congress passes adequate appropriations for the necessary White House entertaining—"

"You should never make such a confession in the hearing of a policeman," said the President with a laugh. "You could be charged with the cold-blooded murder of oenophilia."

"Surely not," said Mrs. Roosevelt. "Only with oenophobia."

"*Touché*, Babs! Very good!"

Mrs. Roosevelt stood, smiling broadly, pleased for once to have been able to take part in the kind of banter her husband loved. She nodded at Kennelly and Szczygiel. "We'll leave you to your deliberations and wish you the best of luck with them."

When Kennelly arrived at the boardinghouse, Mrs. Bogardus was blustering around, recruiting boarders to help her clear the dinner table. No, she said, neither Julie Finch nor Eva Lee was there. "Well . . . it's no skin off my nose," she said. "They pay for their supper whether they eat it or not."

On the front porch a moment later, a small, plump girl approached and spoke to Kennelly. "Eva doesn't have supper here very often. She likes to start her fun early."

"So where can I find her?"

"You know the BB Bar on D? The Ben Butler? She

works at the National Archives, so that's handy for her. If she's not there, somebody there will likely know where she is. Eva loves bars. I don't mean—"

"I didn't suppose you did. Thanks for the info."

He knew the Ben Butler. It had been a popular bar in the old days. Being about halfway between the Capitol and the White House, it was frequented by journalists and lobbyists and a few politicians. It was also near the Gayety Theater, to which many of them would repair for another form of relaxation.

It had been, sequentially, a saloon, a speakeasy, and a post-Prohibition bar. In its saloon days the bartenders had scattered sawdust on the floor, because some customers elected to spit tobacco juice. During Prohibition, women had joined its clientele; and not only did the sawdust disappear, but the spittoons were removed. Sawdust invaded women's little shoes, and cuspidors offended the fair sex. The proprietors had replaced sawdust with peanut shells. Peanuts were served at the bar and on every table, and customers were welcome to cast the shells on the floor. They made a satisfying, somehow dissolute, crunch underfoot.

Other bars had succumbed to spun aluminum, stainless steel, and pink lights. The BB had remained traditional, with heavy oak tables and chairs. Its staple was mugs of beer, sometimes served with shots of whiskey. A long bar ran the whole length of the east side. A buffet was spread in the back, not free as in saloon times but offering substantial sandwiches for twenty cents, a platter consisting of a sandwich, potato salad, and baked beans for fifty cents. A pickle or a deviled egg could be had for a penny. The lights—incandescent bulbs burning in milk-glass shades—did not glare on the drinkers but shed a friendly light on them. Little art was displayed on the walls, except a small collection of ancient circus posters, the value of which no one in the BB ever guessed.

Kennelly knew the BB. The BB knew him. When he stepped up to the bar, the crowd of regulars opened to accommodate him, and a foaming mug of ice-cold beer was pushed toward him before he spoke a word.

"Evenin', Cap'n."

"Evening, Orrin. How's biz?"

"Good. But *different.* Never thought I'd see the day when we could sell more beer than we can buy. An'— Look at 'em, Ed. Ever figure you'd see—?"

He meant, had Ed ever figured he'd see the BB crowded with Government Girls in tight slacks, cozy with young men in the various uniforms of the armed services. And Ed shook his head. No, he'd never figured it.

"Not a cigar goin' in the place," said the bartender. "A hundred cigarettes but—Hey, I can remember when a man smokin' a cigarette was thought of as a sissy. Real men smoked cigars and pipes."

Ed sipped his beer. "I'm looking for a girl, Orrin. A witness, not a suspect. You know a girl named Eva Lee?"

The bartender laughed. "She heard you, Ed!"

Ed turned and faced a grinning girl sitting on the bar. He recognized her. She was the nude photographed by Paul Weyrich: a handsome, slender, sloe-eyed girl dressed in a tight yellow T-shirt and a blue knee-length linen skirt. Her dark-brown hair was straight and was brushed down her back. She had a vaguely Oriental look.

Two young men attended Eva. The length of her skirt and her pose were modest enough; she showed only her knees and an inch or two of stocking-covered leg above, and a brassiere confined her ample breasts against too well-defined an appearance through the T-shirt. On the other hand, she was conspicuously a *fun* girl. That she was perched on the bar said that.

Only girls who were fun sat on bars. She needed only to shift her legs a little to show the bare skin of her legs above her stockings, and Kennelly had no doubt that she did sometimes. It didn't mean she was for sale. It meant only that she would accept a drink from a guy with a good line or a good story. This was how she relieved the boredom of life in an office and a boardinghouse. When a guy suggested they check into a hotel for an hour, she would smile and say no—so firmly that he did not press the matter. There were thousands of these girls in Washington. They were WACS and WAVES, all but a few of them out of uniform. They were clerks and secretaries. They were desperate not to be bored. That was their life. They did important work all day and tried to find a life at night.

This was the kind of girl who troubled the ladies of the

WCTU and DAR, to whom a female entering a bar at all was an offense against public morals. They failed to distinguish between these girls and the hookers on the streets, of whom there were many, or even from the girls who undressed in public on the stage of the Gayety Theater. The Cave Dwellers simply could not understand the Government Girls.

"Miss Lee," said the bartender. "The man who wants to talk to you is Captain Ed Kennelly, DC police."

Ed had only to fix his eyes on her two companions to make them back away, leaving him space to talk to Eva alone.

"I have just one simple question for you, Miss Lee," he said. "Did you receive Miss Finch's mail, find an envelope from Paul Weyrich, and call her to tell her it was at the boardinghouse?"

She nodded. "Absolutely. I called Julie and told her she had a letter from Paul. I knew he was dead, of course."

"This letter was in a stamped envelope with a cancellation on the stamp?"

"Looked like any other letter."

"Was Julie upset to receive this letter?"

"*Upset!* Of course she was upset. The man was *dead!* She read it. It made her more upset. I got a card from *National Geographic* once. It said something like, 'A gift subscription for 1940 has been entered in your name with compliments from "Dad."' My father had been dead six weeks. He'd paid for that subscription before he died. I mean—"

Ed nodded. "I understand. You knew Paul Weyrich fairly well yourself, did you not?"

"We were all friends. Julie was his girl."

"You posed nude for him."

Eva grinned. "That was okay. It was okay because he was . . . Well, he wasn't a professional photographer, but he was a damned advanced amateur. He had an expensive German camera, and he did wonderful, artistic work. He won ribbons for his photos. I'd have been flattered if he'd won a ribbon for any of the pictures he took of me."

"Was Julie jealous about that?"

"Naah. She was there when he took the pictures. When he did pictures of her, she wouldn't take off her last items, but she wasn't jealous. She was kind of dumb about that. Anyway, Paul and I were friends, but *she* was his girl."

Kennelly glanced around. "Can we sit down at a table and talk privately?"

"Hey. I need a lawyer?" Eva asked, half facetiously but not entirely so.

"You don't need a lawyer," said Kennelly. "You're not a suspect. Need another beer?"

Eva glanced at the bartender. "He's got some first-rate Scotch he holds back."

"Orrin . . . ?"

"In shot glasses," said the bartender. "Don't want everybody to know what we've got."

They sat down at a table about halfway back in the saloon. A busy waiter put a fresh bowl of peanuts on the table. Orrin came in a moment, bringing doubles of the single-malt Scotch and glasses of iced seltzer water. "It'd be a sin to water that," he said.

"Never fear," said Eva.

"Tell me about these people."

"Which people? Julie and Paul?"

Kennelly took a spare sip of his Scotch and nodded.

"Julie is a nice girl, really," said Eva. "Maybe she falls in love too easily and too often, but she *does* fall in love. She's not a tramp. Paul . . . Well, Paul was the hard one to judge."

"Meaning?"

"He was loaded with smarts and money. He could have had dates with any girl. So why Julie? She's a nice girl, but she's not what you'd call quality—any more than you'd call *me* quality."

"Eva . . ."

"Hey, man! I came here from South Dakota. If not for the war and . . . Hell. I didn't know what underwear was. I'd never had any. I wore shoes in the winter but not in the summer, when you would wear them out for nothing. It was *crap* to live like I lived, mister—and I didn't even know it. My teacher had made me learn to type. My father had never seen a typewriter and couldn't imagine what it was good for. My brothers are in the service, except one who was killed at Pearl Harbor. The war was our chance to— Die."

"Julie?"

"Not from as bad as I came from. Hell . . . You ever seen a person who *froze to death?* Well, I have. Layin' in the snow and lookin' like he was just as alive as you or me. But frozen. Stiff. Julie's a good girl. I got an idea she went too far with Paul Weyrich, but she's a good girl, from a part of the country where people don't fall down in the snow and just don't get up—they just don't want to all that much. Julie wouldn't know about things like that. But I think she let Paul in her pants."

"She was handy," said Kennelly. "She was his secretary. From what I've read in his letters, I'd say he found her convenient and willing. He was surprised at how far she would go with him. And then he found out they'd gone *too* far."

Eva took some of the unwatered, uniced, single-malt Scotch in her mouth, held it there and savored it for a moment, rolling it around before she swallowed it. "I couldn't figure it," she said. "Julie's a Government Girl, in Washington for the same reason as me: to make some money while the making is good."

"She was married once," said Kennelly. "Her ex-father-in-law is a member of Congress."

"Really! She never said anything about that. Does she . . . does she have kids?"

"No. I don't know. I don't suppose so."

"But she's got political clout, huh?"

"No, not really. Not really."

"Odd. I kind of wondered if there wasn't some political connection between her and Paul. They talked politics a little. Not much, in front of me."

"Saying what?" he asked.

"Well . . . I thought it was kind of funny that a man who worked for President Roosevelt—I mean, worked *directly* for President Roosevelt and talked with him every week at least—could actually despise the man. But despise him he did!"

"Why?"

"I'm not a political person," said Eva, "but he said Roosevelt was another dictator, just like Hitler and Stalin and Mussolini. Julie asked him not to talk that way, think it if he wanted to, but not talk it."

"What did *she* think of the President?"

Eva sipped from her glass and shrugged. "Julie's like me, a nonpolitical person. She's just a kid from Tennessee, come up here to get a job and lucky enough to land one in the White House."

"How you figure she got that lucky?"

"I can tell you one thing. She wasn't seeing Paul before she went to the White House. He didn't hire her because he was sleeping with her, if that's what you've got in mind. I don't know how she got to the White House. Luck of the draw. It could have happened to me."

"Did you ever meet any of Paul's friends?"

She nodded. "It wasn't a very nice kind of meeting. Paul showed his friend some photos of me in the altogether, and that made this guy want to meet me. Hey . . . Not because he thought I was beautiful or anything, just because I'd posed nude. Paul invited him to his apartment, and he invited Julie and me. All this guy could think of was Paul taking some more pictures, while he watched. I wouldn't do it, and the guy almost cried. You know, I don't think he had it in mind that he wanted to go to bed with me or anything like that. All he wanted was to see me naked. Creep!"

"What was this friend's name?"

"Pipe. Ross T. Pipe. With that name and because his hair had been red before he went bald, he was bound to be called Rusty. He liked it. Rusty Pipe."

"Did *he* talk politics?"

"Sort of. He and Paul talked about the way things would be after 'the big change.' I asked what big change they had in mind, and both of them just smiled and said a big change was coming."

"How were things going to be after the big change?"

"The *people* were going to govern. I suspected they were Communists."

"Did you ever see him after that one time at Weyrich's apartment?"

"Believe it or not, the guy called me and said he'd like to take me to dinner at a first-class restaurant. He said he'd offended me and hadn't meant to, and he'd like me to see he wasn't a bad fellow. I went to dinner with him. Funny . . . J. Edgar Hoover and his boyfriend were at a table very close to ours. Anyway, Rusty said the idea of seeing me naked had excited him too much and made him offensive, for which he apologized. He said if I'd see him from time to time he would never suggest anything of the kind again. He'd treat me with respect, he said. So I've had dinner with him, I guess three more times; and he's always treated me with respect. So much respect it's embarrassing. He's still a creep, but I guess he's the kind of creep a girl can tolerate for a while."

"What about the big change?"

She shook her head. "He never talked about it again, except to say the world couldn't go on the way it was and things had to be made different. I tell ya, Captain. I've got so I feel sorry for Rusty. He's one of those lonesome guys that can't quite make it in life. I've let him kiss me on the porch of the boardinghouse, a couple of times. He's so grateful that your heart goes out to him."

"Where does he work?"

"Oh, at the Pentagon Building. He always wears civvies, but I figure he's an officer of some kind."

VII

THE FIRST LADY LEFT the White House shortly after 7:00 P.M. A War Bond rally was being held in the ballroom of the Mayflower Hotel. It would feature an auction of items belonging to celebrity donors. She herself was taking a black straw hat in which she had been photographed on many occasions. To be admitted and allowed to bid, a guest had to show $1,000 worth of war bonds. The proceeds of the auction went to the purchase of more war bonds, which would be owned by the successful bidders and would be redeemable in 1953.

Some of the donors would not be present. Clark Gable, for example, who was serving in the armed forces, had sent a white silk scarf he had worn in a picture featuring him as a suave playboy type. Jimmy Stewart, similarly, sent the necktie he had worn on the Senate floor in *Mr. Smith Goes to Washington.* Claudette Colbert sent a string of faux pearls that had been part of one of her costumes when she played Cleopatra. Each of the Marx brothers had sent a memento. Groucho's donation was a pair of round spectacles with no lenses. Chico sent a conical hat he wore as part of his Italian costume. Harpo sent a horn that could be tooted with a rubber bulb. W. C. Fields sent a boater straw hat he had worn in *You Can't Cheat an Honest Man*. Bela Lugosi sent a white bow tie, part of his costume as Count Dracula.

The focus of the auction was Hollywood personalities, and the master of ceremonies was to be Cecil B. DeMille. Told that the First Lady was in the room, he strode toward her, beaming.

"An auspicious evening," said the most famous film director in Hollywood, the creator of overblown, tacky biblical extravaganzas—a man, however, with a sure finger on the pulse of public taste. "I can't say how grateful we are to see you here."

"I am most pleased to be here, Mr. DeMille," said Mrs. Roosevelt.

"Let me present someone who is glad to see you again. I believe you know Humphrey Bogart."

Bogart had approached just behind DeMille and was indeed conspicuously pleased to see the First Lady.

For all his tough-guy roles, Bogart was actually the mannerly son of a Park Avenue family. His father was a surgeon, his mother a professional photographer who sold pictures of her son to an advertising campaign for baby food. He had served in the navy in the First World War, and a wound taken when a shell hit his ship had scarred and partially paralyzed his lip—the source of the notorious Bogart sneer.

"It's a real pleasure, ma'am. We met when you were in California visiting Elliott," said Bogart.

"I remember it well, Mr. Bogart. I remember it very well."

Bogart, who usually let his cigarette dangle from a corner of his mouth, held it between his fingers at his left side now. Since she last saw him he had developed a reputation for drinking heavily—though that might have been just gossip; gossip being next to motion pictures the most ostentatious product of Hollywood.

"I've seen Elliott since," said Bogart. "At a party given by Howard Hughes at his villa in the hills. I can compliment Elliot, ma'am. When he saw what kind of party it was, he was out of there pretty quick."

"What sort of party was it, Mr. Bogart?"

Bogart smiled. "Oh, nothing so bad. Not an orgy, certainly. It was centered on his pool and cabanas. Some of the girls were nude in the water. Some sat around in their underthings. I actually don't think Howard Hughes would have stood for anything . . . well, you know. But Elliott, I guess, saw right off that it was nowhere for a son of the President to be in wartime when other sons were— You know what I mean."

"Elliott," said Mrs. Roosevelt, "had come home briefly from North Africa to examine an airplane Mr. Hughes hoped to sell to the government, to replace the P-38, which seems not to operate well in cold climates. Elliott flies a P-38 and is aware of its merits and deficiencies. His recommendation, I believe, was that the government allow Lockheed to improve the P-38, which they said they could do in a few months, rather than replace it with an airplane Mr. Hughes said he would need a year or more to develop fully and test."

"I had a drink with him later, before he went back to war," said Bogart. "He explained it just as you have said it. I didn't ask him why he had departed from the Hughes party abruptly, but I think he used good judgment."

"Elliott has not invariably used good judgment," said the First lady. "But the President and I trust him and are proud of him."

"We are," said DeMille grandiloquently, "about to be descended on by that disreputable viper Hedda Hopper."

Hollywood's preeminent gossip columnist, she of the flamboyant hats and the poison pen was indeed easing her way toward them, wearing a toothy smile that could have lighted the room.

"You want to silence her," said Bogart, "you serve her a drink. Mix it with lighter fluid. She'll drink it; she won't know the difference. And coming home she'll fall down short of her door. She's been found boozy asleep on her front lawn, many a sunrise. Many a nasty story has been killed that way—because she won't remember what she had in mind to write."

"I suppose I can't escape her," said Mrs. Roosevelt.

"Just don't tell her anything," said Bogart. "I'll watch her. If I see she's putting together some lies, I'll booze her up and dump her in a fountain somewhere."

Hedda Hopper was indeed already a little bit tipsy. Her smile was too broad. Her eyes were too wide and seemed not to remain focused. She was as usual wearing heavy makeup, inexpertly applied.

"*Mrs. Roosevelt!* What an *honor!*" She blinked. "C. B., Bogie. Oh, Mrs. R, you simply *must* tell me about Elliott and the Howard Hughes pool party. I've heard so many versions. What did happen actually? I can't write a word about it until I know the truth."

"When did a little thing like the truth ever discourage you?" sneered Bogart.

"Now, Bogie, I've treated *you* with a great deal of restraint. Anyway— The party. The word is that it was an *orgy*."

"Ask someone who was there," said Bogart.

"Who?"

"Me. *I* was there."

"Well . . . ?"

"Well, a couple of girls decided to take off their clothes and swim nude. Three or four others stripped down to their undies and sat around on the deck. Wasn't it Shakespeare who wrote, 'Two swimming nudes and four undies-clad sojourners doth not an orgy make'? Wasn't it?"

"What about Elliott, then?"

Bogart smiled the distorted smile his wound had caused. "*Venit, vidit, exit,*" to paraphrase Caesar. "He came, he saw, he left. When Elliott saw the naked girls, he shook hands with Hughes, thanked him for the invitation, and left."

"I must say, that's a bit disappointing," said Hedda.

"I suppose it is," said Bogart. "As for me, '*Veni, vidi, mani.*' I came, I saw, I stayed. It was no orgy, but it was my kind of party."

When the First Lady returned to the White House, the Trident Conference was still in session. In her study she found some telephone notes from Tommy, but it was too late to return those calls tonight. She went to bed.

Friday morning dawned rainy in Washington. Mrs. Roosevelt was up early, answered some of last evening's calls, and dictated some correspondence. As she looked out her windows, the Washington Monument was all but obscured by the rain.

Ed Kennelly called, and about nine-thirty he arrived at the White House. Stan Szczygiel joined him and the First Lady in her study. She sent for coffee and pastries.

"Have you gotten the information yet, Stan?" Ed asked.

"Yes. Major Ross T. Pipe is with the Corps of Engineers, United States Army. Before he entered the army he was a civil engineer. He came in from the Illinois National Guard and was assigned to the engineers at the request of

Congressman Everett Dirksen. He came in as a captain in 1941 and has been promoted once. His assignment . . ." Szczygiel paused significantly, raised his chin, and said, "His assignment is the security of government buildings. As an experienced civil engineer, he knows what is under the streets; he knows what you find when you go down a manhole. Since 1941, the Corps of Engineers, acting in concert with Army Intelligence, has filled in a hundred or more old tunnels under the streets of Washington. They have blocked others with steel barricade doors. In still others, they have stationed guards. The rule is, if a tunnel is not being used it is filled in or blocked. It used to be possible to crawl through nasty old tunnels and get from here to there to some other place in downtown Washington. No more."

"Uhh . . . The significance?" asked Mrs. Roosevelt.

"Sorry," said Ed Kennelly. "We haven't told you yet, but Major Pipe was a personal friend of Paul Weyrich. Not only that. He talked with Weyrich about how different things would be after what the two of them called a 'big change.' "

"That sounds like Communist talk," she said.

Ed nodded. "What's more, he's socially inept, according to Eva Lee, who's been dating him."

"Eva is . . . ?"

"Julie's friend, who posed nude for Weyrich."

"Oh, yes. Does that fact have any significance?" asked the First Lady.

"Probably not."

Mrs. Roosevelt smiled gently. "When I was a girl it would have had great significance," she said. "We supposed that girls who did that were of the lowest possible character. Now . . . How did Cole Porter put it? 'Now, God knows, anything goes.' "

Stan Szczygiel spoke almost as if he had not heard this last exchange. "So Pipe, who knows the infrastructure of the city, was a friend of Weyrich, who smuggled a gun into the White House. And both of them talked about a big change. I find that suggestive."

"Of an assassination plot?" asked the First Lady.

"In the Secret Service we have to think about that all the time," said Stan. "Lincoln was assassinated. Garfield was assassinated. McKinley was assassinated. A shot was fired at President Theodore Roosevelt after he left office but was campaigning to return. One was fired at President-elect Franklin Roosevelt. Booth was a conspirator. Guiteau was a nut. Czolgolsz was a nut. Schrank was a nut. Zangara was a nut. We've got nuts to worry about today. But, worse, we've got conspirators—Nazis, Communists, and . . . we can't forget the old Roosevelt-haters. Damn them; they're still around, and they wouldn't shrink from murder."

Mrs. Roosevelt sighed loudly and shook her head. "Think of it. To assassinate the President while the Prime Minister is here—"

"Or to assassinate the Prime Minister in the White House," said Szczygiel.

They paused as the First Lady poured coffee and served little pastries.

"We know one thing for sure," said Kennelly. "And that is that Julie has lied to us. She said she went with Weyrich to the conference room—and she didn't. In my experience as an investigator I can tell you that just one lie is significant. Motive? Why would she lie about that? And that letter from Weyrich, supposedly almost posthumously. Eva confirms that it did come in the mail to their boardinghouse. But she doesn't know if it came from the White House. What says it wasn't mailed Wednesday from somewhere in downtown Washington? We don't have the envelope, which she conveniently left in a taxicab."

"It was in fact typed on Weyrich's typewriter," said Stan. "We enlarged the type and could see that."

"A typewriter to which Julie had access," said Kennelly firmly.

"What are you suggesting, Ed?" asked Mrs. Roosevelt.

"I suggest we arrest her, lock her up, and let her sweat. That brings the truth out."

"But surely—"

"Well . . . She might be more useful outside than in. Let me suggest something. Suppose I have her arrested this morning, lock her up for the rest of the day and overnight, and let her go in the morning. Let her have a taste of the slammer. It might put her in a mood to cooperate."

"Do you think that is really necessary? What do you hope she will say?" asked Mrs. Roosevelt.

"The next key in this mystery is Rusty Pipe," said Kennelly, not responding to the First Lady's questions. "I bet ya anything Rusty can tell us something useful."

Major Ross Pipe was an unprepossessing man, perhaps thirty-five years old, slight of stature, bald, with a small bland face that tended in repose to settle into a reserved quizzical smile. Eva had said she had never seen him in uniform, but he was in uniform now: the uniform of a National Guard captain called to active service and assigned to the Pentagon—meaning that his chest was not burdened with ribbons for overseas service, or for heroism, not even one for marksmanship.

He welcomed Ed Kennelly into his little office with an artificial show of cordiality, pointed to a chair, and offered a cigarette from a wooden box.

Kennelly accepted the cigarette and a light, and Pipe lit one for himself.

"You want to speak to me about Paul Weyrich," said Pipe. "I'll gladly answer any question I can, but I'm afraid I won't be able to be of much help."

"How long did you know him?"

"I suppose I knew him about fifteen years, in the sense of being an acquaintance. We were students at the University of Chicago about the same time, you see. When he came to Washington—that was in the fall of 1940—he called me for assistance in finding housing. I'd just gone through the ordeal of finding a place to live myself, and I was able to help him. We became friends: two old Chicago boys in a strange city."

"What do you know about his relationship with Julie Finch?"

Pipe grinned. "Paul was very awkward about girls," he said. "As I am, myself. To be frank, I doubt he'd ever had . . . uh, intercourse before he did it with Julie. Of course, she's an innocent girl-child from, I think, Tennessee; and she was flattered that he would want her."

"What about Eva?"

"Eva is . . . not the same. Eva is far more sophisticated."

"Did Weyrich have intercourse with her?"

"No. I'm really sure he didn't."

"Have you?"

The major winced. "Do I have to answer?"

"No, you don't have to answer," said Kennelly. He tapped some ash into the glass ashtray on Pipe's desk. "Unless you want to."

"Well . . . Alright, I *do* want to. The answer is yes, I do. But I'm afraid I'm not the only one who does."

"Why do you say that?"

Pipe frowned and shook his head. "I wish I *hadn't* said it. A gentleman shouldn't— she's a simple, lively girl. So is Julie. Just innocent kids who came to Washington to be Government Girls."

Kennelly decided to try another approach. "What do you know about Weyrich's politics?"

Pipe shrugged. "Nothing in particular."

"What was the 'big change' he talked about."

The major blanched. "I . . . I never heard him say anything about a big change. Maybe he was talking about the end of the war and—"

"Maybe he was," Kennelly interrupted. "Maybe he was. I understand you are involved in closing off unnecessary tunnels and conduits under the chief government buildings."

"Yes. There's a remarkable underground tangle beneath downtown Washington. Many of the old tunnels are no longer in use."

"A couple of years ago," said Kennelly, "the Secret Service closed a drainage tunnel that ran under East Executive Avenue. Coming through that, a man could get inside the fence and be on the White House grounds."

"I know. That was before we began a systematic examination of the infrastructure."

"Are there still ways to enter?"

"I believe there are none. We've closed three others since 1941. The White House is easy. You should see what was under the Capitol. You haven't smelled anything until you smell sewage that's been in a wet tunnel a hundred years and more. The guys who closed that tunnel wore respirators, which made it possible for them to joke. Like, 'Suppose this is Daniel Webster's? Or Henry Clay's?' Ugghh!"

Back at his office, Ed Kennelly sat down at an Underwood typewriter and wrote out a note to himself. He used carbon paper to make a copy for Mrs. Roosevelt and one for Stan Szczygiel.

```
CONTRADICTIONS—
J F says she and W went to the conference
room to deliver documents. Prez says
didn't.
   Maj. P says he has intercourse with
Eva. Eva says doesn't.
   Eva says W talked about big change.
Maj. P says didn't.
   Why nobody knows about J's political
connections? Eva doesn't know. P doesn't,
it looks like. Why hide?
   Motive for lying. Eva? P? Julie.
```

Paul Weyrich's body was released by the coroner on Wednesday afternoon, and on Friday his father and brother arrived in Washington to claim it and put it on a train for Chicago. The President asked Mrs. Roosevelt to call on the Weyrichs and express his regrets and hers. She went to the funeral home, where a few Washington friends had gathered to view the body and extend their sympathy. This duty, and ones much like it, was one of the most difficult burdens she had to bear.

The father wept when he saw she had come. When he recovered his composure, he said, "I can't imagine what happened to my son, Mrs. Roosevelt, but I do imagine, when all the facts can be told, it will be recognized that he died serving his country."

She nodded. "I don't know what happened either, Mr. Weyrich, but I wouldn't be surprised if what you just said proves exactly right."

She took a moment to look at the guest register before they left and saw that Julie Finch, Major Ross T. Pipe, and Eva Lee had called and signed the register—apparently together.

When she returned to the White House she had a number of calls to return. One was from Congressman Lawrence Mellon. He asked if she could spare him a few minutes. She asked Tommy to call him and say she would spare him as much time as he wanted, anytime that afternoon. He arrived at the White House a little after four, and Mrs. Roosevelt received him in the President's oval study.

Congressman Mellon was a Southern politician of the old style. He was one of the last members of Congress to wear a wing collar. As he would have explained it, he was at pains to be what his constituents wanted: dramatically a congressman, traditional in speech and manner, conservative on matters of mores and morals, liberal in matters that involved benefits for his district. He was white-haired, flush-faced, jowly. For the nonce he was not smoking a cigar, though a cigar in his hand or mouth was an essential element of his persona.

"I find myself in the most embarrassing of circumstances," he said as soon as pleasantries had been exchanged. He spoke with a patrician's air and a Southerner's accent.

"Oh, I hope not," said the First Lady.

"I am afraid so," he said. "I have had a telephone call from someone I had hoped I would not hear from again. I refer to my son's former wife, who calls herself Julie Finch. She called me from the District jail, tearfully complaining that she is confined there. I demanded an explanation, of course, and she asked me to contact you, saying you knew all about her trouble and could explain it and probably secure her release. The matter involves, I suppose, the death of Paul Weyrich."

"I don't believe, Congressman, that she is suspected of having killed Mr. Weyrich. I believe she is suspected of having been less than truthful when she was asked certain questions."

"Figures," he said, nodding solemnly. "Truthful is something she never was."

"Tell me about her," said Mrs. Roosevelt.

"Well . . . I don't suppose you'll like the term much, but Julie comes from what we in the South call 'poor white trash.' They never amounted to nothin', the Finches. Her father sold corn squeezin's—still does, I suppose. He never amounted to anything, but he was *smart.* He could always figure a way to turn a dollar without working hard for it. She inherited that. Julie is smart. Too damned smart. Don't let her cry and plead she's never been in jail before and can't stand it. She's been in before. For shoplifting."

"Now . . . She was married to your son—"

"My son, Lawrence Mellon Jr. can be a boob about some things. I want him to have a political career, but he has to learn a lot of things I guess I never had to learn; they just came instinctively to me. Anyway, when this pretty white-trash girl came along, he couldn't resist her. The first thing you know, he's got her pregnant. He had to marry her. But it wouldn't do, you know. She was too much the tramp. So we got the divorce. It was after that she winds up in jail for shoplifting in the five-and-dime. But it could have been for selling her dad's moonshine. I wanted her out of town, out of Tennessee. I asked Harry Hopkins to find her a job in Washington, and I got the charges against her dropped on condition she move to Washington and never come back. Now, if she's involved in a murder—"

"Congressman. We are trying to keep confidential for the moment the fact that there has been a murder in the White House. Mr. Churchill is here, as you know—"

"Mum's the word with me, ma'am. It's Julie's mouth you had better worry about."

"I feel sorry for her, being in the DC jail. It's not a pleasant place, and I know it's frightening, too. But I think I can assure you that she will be released in the morning."

"Don't feel too sorry for her. Jail doesn't scare her. She spent fifteen days in jail back home. And you know what she said? She said she guessed everybody in a lifetime had to do a little time behind bars. It was just a part of life."

VIII

SATURDAY MORNING WAS NO different from any other morning in the White House routine. Mrs. Roosevelt dictated two newspaper columns and some letters and returned some phone calls.

Then she dressed in a summery pleated white dress and went down to the Private Dining Room for a special breakfast. Her guest was Grace Coolidge, First Lady during the administration of her late husband Calvin Coolidge.

Grace Coolidge had been the First Lady that Mrs. Roosevelt sometimes wished she could be. Handsome, lithe, stylish, voluble, witty, she had left the White House as one of the most popular women in America. During the thirties she had won several awards for having made valuable contributions to education in America. In her early sixties now, she was still an appealing, personable woman. Mrs. Roosevelt saw her rarely, but when she did they were cordial.

They talked mostly about the war, but Mrs. Coolidge

had something to say about the White House. "What is the line attributed to Bette Davis?" she asked. "Looking at a house for the first time—in one of her pictures, of course—she said, 'What . . . a . . . *dump!*' Well, that's the White House. If it is not soon thoroughly remodeled, it is simply going to fall down. I know the problem. The Congress won't appropriate the funds to give the Presidents a luxurious mansion, and none of the Presidents has felt he could press on the matter."

"My husband has pointed out the problem to committees, but they have never moved," said Mrs. Roosevelt.

"Well, you are fortunate. You are on the move all the time and don't have to sit in the place and brood. *My* husband, you know, didn't even want me to attend White House social functions."

"It was a good thing you did," said Mrs. Roosevelt. "Poor Mr. Coolidge was *so* awkward."

"He wasn't Silent Cal by choice," said Grace Coolidge with a wry smile. "He was silent because every time he opened his mouth he stuck his foot in it."

"My husband did not often agree with him," said Mrs. Roosevelt, "but he held President Coolidge in high personal regard."

"I was married to the man for twenty-eight years. *I* held him in high personal regard. He valued probity above all other values. I have to say, I think he valued it too much."

• • •

After assuring Grace Coolidge that she would always be welcome at the White House, Mrs. Roosevelt returned to her study, where she found a glum Julie Finch waiting in the custody of Ed Kennelly.

"Ed . . . I assume you have asked Miss Finch the questions you wanted to ask her. Why don't you let me talk to her alone?"

Kennelly stood. "Why not?"

"Do I have to go back to jail?" Julie asked tearfully.

"That's going to depend on whether or not you tell the truth," said Kennelly. "Don't suppose we know nothing about this case except what you've told us. When your story contradicts someone else's story, we have to remember that you lied during your first statements to us. For now . . . you can go back to work or go home."

With a farewell smile at the First Lady, Kennelly left.

Mrs. Roosevelt looked closely at Julie Finch. The girl was bedraggled. She looked as though she had slept in her clothes: a simple dark-blue dress with a red patent-leather belt. Her hair was tousled. She wore no makeup. She sat slumped.

"Have you had coffee?"

"What they call coffee."

The First Lady picked up the phone and ordered coffee and pastries, posthaste.

"This means I'm out of a job, I suppose," said Julie.

"As a matter of fact, I spoke briefly with the President about that. Mr. Weyrich has to be replaced. His successor may want to bring his own secretary. Whether he does or doesn't, you can remain to introduce him or his new secretary to the pending work. After that . . . well, we shall see. The President can't even think about that until the current conference is over."

"I 'ppreciate that."

"You understand that you are in possession of extremely confidential information. You know a vital conference is in session, and you know who is here for it. If you were to reveal any of that, you would be sent to the federal reformatory for women for a very long term."

"I am an honest person," Julie said simply.

"I am afraid you are not, entirely. What Captain Kennelly just said is true. You lied to us on Wednesday. Maybe you thought you had reason. But it has to stop now."

"I loved Paul," Julie murmured.

"Very well, but let's discuss some things you have not told the truth about. In the first place, yesterday afternoon and last night was not your first experience of jail. Did you not spend fifteen days in jail in Tennessee, for shoplifting?"

"In a rat-infested iron *cage*, with plumbin' that didn't work, and no bed. I slept on the *floor*. To feed me, they scraped the plates from the sheriff's table and brought me platters of stuff that had already been nibbled on. Which my dear daddy-in-law has told you all about. Well . . . I was in two other times that he doesn't know about—for gettin' drunk and gettin' in fights. The Mellons didn't know me then. I was kind of a wild girl before I met Larry Mellon and got married, and I was kind of a wild girl again after they broke up my marriage and took my baby away from me. Figure *that one*, Mrs. Roosevelt. I straightened up and was a good enough wife to Larry, but the Mellons didn't want me and made him believe he didn't either. They ran me out of town finally, is what they did. They sent me to Washin'ton, where my gaudy ol' daddy-in-law fixed it up for me to have a job here in the White House. Congressman Lawrence Mellon can smooth over anything. He's a smooth one, he is. I couldn't even type. He sent me to typin' school, so I could work in Washin'ton and live in a boardinghouse. If he'd had any influence with Admiral Byrd, he'd have arranged for me to go to Antarctica!"

Mrs. Roosevelt drew a deep breath. "All I am interested in is in learning who killed Paul Weyrich and why. I believe you know more than you have told."

"Ask me questions. I'll answer."

"Mr. Weyrich, talked about a 'big change' coming. What did he mean by that?"

"He meant . . . He meant that pretty soon the war was going to be over and then big changes were coming."

"Like what?"

"Well . . . A more democratic way of doing things."

"The Communist way?"

"I suppose you could say that."

"Do you mean to say that Mr. Weyrich was a Communist?"

"I . . . don't think I could call him that. He was just a very deep thinker who didn't like the way things are run in this country and thought things could be better."

"Who else thought that way?"

"Well . . . I guess I did, maybe. I've been pushed around pretty hard, Mrs. Roosevelt. You've never been in jail. You don't know what that's like. You can't *imagine* what it's like. Well . . . I have. I've been chained up and locked up. And there's lots of us who have. I was in jail with a nigger woman who told me she'd spent half her life in jail, for doing nothing, just for being a nigger. Well . . . They talk that way, but I got so I believed her. Even those plates of leftover food . . . I got mine first, and she got what was left. I got so I left more than I ate. Well, okay— You've never had a baby taken away from you. *I* have. I've been crapped on, ma'am. I love my country, but I don't figure I owe much to the way things are run in this country."

"What about Major Ross Pipe? Did he think that way?"

"Rusty! I doubt Rusty ever thinks at all. He's not bright."

"How did Mr. Weyrich get a gun into the White House? Captain Kennelly can't carry his police sidearm into the White House."

"I told you. I don't think he did. I think that gun was planted on him after he was dead."

The coffee and pastry was delivered, and the First Lady poured for Julie. "You said you and Mr. Weyrich stopped at the conference room, where he delivered a folder of papers the President had asked for. The President says he never asked for any papers and that Mr. Weyrich never came to the room. That was a lie, Miss Finch."

"I'll tell you the same thing I told Kennelly. He pressed me about it last night. I told that lie because I was real embarrassed by why we came into the White House that night. I told you about the Red Room."

"What you told us was not true."

"Maybe I can prove it's true."

"How?"

"Can we go to the Red Room? I left something there."

Reluctantly Mrs. Roosevelt accompanied Julie to the Red Room. There Julie dropped to her hands and knees, reached up under a settee, and pulled a pair of white rayon panties out of the springs.

"See. I told you we came here. Paul thought it would be a big joke to tuck these up inside a piece of furniture. They might not be found in this century, he said, but whoever found them would wonder what was goin' on in the White House when they were put there."

"So that's why you came into the White House that night," said the First Lady. "To experience intimacy in one of the state rooms. That was the only reason?"

"That was all the reason *I* had," said Julie. "I have no idea why Paul went on up to the Lincoln Bedroom."

Mrs. Roosevelt telephoned Ed Kennelly to tell him. He had a report for her, too—

"The lab has finished its examination of Weyrich's typewriter," he told her. They had removed his typewriter from his office and taken it in to be checked for fingerprints or other evidence. "It's covered with fingerprints, absolutely covered with fingerprints, and every last damned one of them is his. What's more, not a single key has been wiped. She didn't use his typewriter and wipe her own prints off the keys."

"And the letter was typed on that typewriter, for sure?"

"Absolutely. Like any other typewriter, that Remington has its signature—blurred letters, misaligned letters, and so on. The letter was typed on that machine and no other."

"Then we must conclude that Mr. Weyrich wrote a farewell letter to Miss Finch: the one she showed us, the one we photostated."

"I don't see any way around it," said Kennelly.

In 1943 most of Washington worked a five-and-a-half-day week. Agencies directly involved in the war and some others besides worked six days, some of them seven; but most federal employees went home at noon on Saturday.

Ed Kennelly had put tails on all the witnesses and suspects he had—Julie Finch, Eva Lee, and Major Ross Pipe—just to see if any of them would do anything quirky. It was a long shot, but it was all he had.

Julie Finch went directly to her boardinghouse. She had said that after a night in jail she wanted to take a bath, and presumably she did.

Eva Lee went home, too, but shortly left to shop in a Woolworth store, then returned to the boardinghouse.

Pipe went home to his apartment, then went out shopping for groceries and returned shortly.

All very normal. Nothing significant. Then Kennelly's tails began to call in other reports—

Julie and Eva left the boardinghouse about three o'clock and went together to Pipe's apartment. They were joined there half an hour later by an unidentified man. The four of them were together in the apartment for an hour, after which Julie left in the company of the unidentified man, who drove her home in his car. Eva remained in Pipe's apartment for the next two hours, after which they left in a cab for dinner, where oddly enough they once more sat at a table very near to the one where J. Edgar Hoover and Clyde Tolson were dining.

Kennelly decided their dinner hour would be a good time to enter Pipe's apartment. This time he did not secure a search warrant. He used a skeleton key and entered the apartment alone.

Pipe did not live as well as Weyrich had. This apartment had been rented furnished, by the look of it, and had the quality of a room in a not-very-expensive hotel.

A recently used condom in a waste basket in the bedroom settled the question of whether or not Pipe was a meticulously respectful gentleman, as he had insisted, or had bedded down with Eva Lee.

Nothing else in the apartment was suggestive of anything—except one thing: Pipe too had a copy of the Elizabeth Dilling book, *The Roosevelt Red Record and Its Background: A Handbook for Patriots*. Mrs. Dilling was still an active Roosevelt-hater, and Kennelly had seen her picture in a newspaper only recently: at some sort of rally, her right arm upraised in the stiff-arm Nazi salute. There was talk that she and some others would soon be indicted for sedition.

Kennelly reported to Mrs. Roosevelt. "My guys got the license number of the car that took Julie home. A Virginia number. We'll have the identification within an hour or two."

Stan Szczygiel came to the First Lady's study early in the afternoon. Besides a file, he was carrying a large cardboard carton. Inside it was the trash basket from Weyrich's office: a fat-hourglass-shaped receptacle made of steel mesh.

"Routine," said Szczygiel. "As a matter of routine we locked all his files and the drawers of his desk, and we even took his trash basket and sealed it in a box. I've put in a great many hours, reading his files— all routine stuff relating to his job. Those routine letters and memos do tell something about the man, though." He handed her a carbon copy of a memorandum to the President. "Read the last paragraph."

> I hope, sir, you will forgive me for interjecting a personal note; but I cannot forbear noting that my work is made immeasurably more difficult by the open hostility of Secretary Hull. I hope it is not petty of me to report that I am unable to reach any conclusion other

than that the man takes a personal dislike to me.

Would it be possible for you to speak to the secretary? If he finds some specific defect in my work or some deficiency in my person, I will endeavor to make any reasonable correction to meet his objections. I cannot, however, work closely with a man who treats me with undefined antipathy and will afford me no opportunity to win his approbation.

Mrs. Roosevelt shook her head. "Cordell Hull? I can't imagine, unless Mr. Weyrich deeply offended him in some way."

"Well . . . The secretary of state is not the only one Weyrich imagined did not like him. Here's a carbon of a letter."

The letter was to Dean Acheson. It discussed several legal issues relative to the transfer of PT boats to the Soviet Union, then went on—

Have I, Dean, in some way offended you? I thought the tone of your criticism of my draft was unnecessarily harsh and personal. If I have offended you, please be so good as to tell me how, so that I may make amends if possible. I had supposed we are friends as well as colleagues.

"There are other letters and memos along the same line," Szczygiel told the First Lady. "They suggest to me that Weyrich was emotionally unstable."

"Why have you brought me his trash basket?"

"I had glanced through what was in it but put it aside while I was exploring his files. This morning I came on this. I looked for the other pages or pages. I've looked everywhere. I guess he didn't think this page was important enough to destroy."

The letter and memorandum she had already seen were carbon copies on onionskin paper. This was an original, on bond paper. It had been crumpled and tossed in the trash basket. Szczygiel had unfolded it.

> If you read this, I will have failed. Or maybe not failed entirely. Succeeded and then failed. We are not fanatics or fools. We are some of America's best. I have

Following that last word was a hole in the page. The typist had made an error and had used an eraser so unskillfully that he had rubbed a hole in the paper. The beginning of a letter, with a hole in the paper, carried a vivid image: of a man highly annoyed to have rubbed a hole in his important letter, tearing it out of the typewriter, wadding it into a ball, and slamming it into the trash.

• • •

The Trident Conference continued. It seemed appropriate to the President and Mrs. Roosevelt that on Saturday evening the conferees have an informal dinner, which she should attend. It was not to be a state dinner. It would be served in the Private Dining Room, to the President and Prime Minister, their chief aides, and their ladies. Kay Summersby would not have been invited, except that Sarah Churchill said firmly that she would not attend either if Kay were excluded. The President had sent a firm order to Mrs. Nesbitt that French champagne and claret were to be served—no New York State mucilage.

Everyone gathered for the President's cocktail hour, including the First Lady, who sipped sherry and tried to take part in the banter.

Before they went down to dinner she took a moment with the President alone in his bedroom.

"I've read a memorandum from Mr. Weyrich to you, in which he complains of the 'hostility' of Secretary Hull."

"Weyrich was a sensitive soul," said the President. "But his work was inestimable. I suggested to Cordell that he treat the young man with kid gloves."

"There are other memoranda and letters in his files in which he protests that his work is underappreciated and friendship is being withheld from him. It all suggests an unstable personality."

The President shrugged. "Well, he's not unstable now, is he?"

"Franklin . . . He may have been involved in a plot to assassinate you, or Mr. Churchill."

"Plot failed," said the President insouciantly.

"It hasn't yet," she said. "Until we find out who was behind it."

Franklin Roosevelt's outward insouciance and exuberance had rarely failed him, ever. She knew the presidency was nowhere near as easy for him as he made it look. Now, suddenly, she saw something she had almost never seen, and it troubled her. For a moment, just a moment, he crumbled. His chin dropped. He closed his eyes. For that quick moment she saw him as an *aging* man, worn down by life and duty. Just for a moment. His head snapped up. His eyes hardened.

"Don't think of it," she said. "The White House Hawkshaw can take care of it. I'm an amateur, but I have excellent professional help."

He nodded. "Our guests . . ."

"Enjoy the wine," she said. "It is not New York State mucilage."

IX

WINSTON CHURCHILL FAVORED SLEEPING late, followed by a leisurely hour in the tub, where he enjoyed a luxury Americans enjoyed daily if they wanted to but was all but unknown in wartime Britain: unlimited hot water. He soaked, smoked a cigar or two, sipped brandy, and read newspapers. He laid a board across the rim of the tub, and that was all that covered him when—as often happened—someone came in to talk to him while he was soaking. It was not uncommon for young female secretaries to sit on chairs by the tub and take dictation. They placed their chairs to afford him such modesty as he had; he made no concessions of his own.

He was not eccentric, particularly. He was simply an Englishman who had been born to an aristocratic way of life, and an element of that way of life was that servants—and to his class secretaries were servants—were assumed blind and deaf. The lord of the manor could say anything in front of his servants, imagining that they did not hear and would not in any case understand what they heard. Servants drew baths. Servants fetched towels, and if they happened to see my lord or my lady naked, well—it was of no great consequence.

Churchill enjoyed long baths, cigars, and brandy. He had achieved what he had achieved without surrendering the pleasures of life, and he saw no reason why he should surrender them. Washington afforded them better than London right now, and he determined to make the best of the opportunities offered him.

On Sunday morning he broke his habit and rose and dressed early enough to join the Roosevelts for religious services in the East Room. In past visits he had gone to church with them, but this time that was not possible because his presence in Washington was a deep secret. On this Sunday, chairs were placed in rows, each with a hymn book, a lectern was set up; and on it was placed the Roosevelt family Bible on which the President had taken the oath of office three times. No provision was made for kneeling. The minister had indicated he would not ask for it.

The conferees assembled, most of them. Staff who had flown in from London were there. White House staff who were party to the secret were present.

The First Lady wore a pink cotton dress and a white straw hat with a small veil that covered only her forehead. The President sat in his wheelchair in an unusually rumpled suit. The Prime Minister was natty in a suit that looked Saville Row—though Mrs. Roosevelt knew his tailor was P.

C. Crowe of Lime Street in the City. General Eisenhower looked uncomfortable in a gray double-breasted suit almost as wrinkled as the President's. General Marshall was not in the least uncomfortable in a well-tailored dark-brown suit. Only General Sir Alan Brooke was in uniform: the crisp summer khaki of the British army.

Mrs. Roosevelt, who had heard him do it before, looked forward so much to hearing the Prime Minister sing a particular hymn that she had asked the Reverend MacAllister to include it in the service. When the time came, she nudged the President and joined him in being amused as the words came out—

Oh, God, our help in ages past,
Our hope for years to co-o-o-me,
Protector from the stormy . . . blarst,
And our eternal home.

It was how they sang it in the Royal Navy, she'd been told.

On Saturday night Ed Kennelly had received from Virginia an identification for the license plate number his officer had taken from the car and had brought the unknown man to the meeting with Julie Finch, Eva Lee, and Rusty Pipe. He had felt too tired to launch an entirely new element of the investigation and had let the matter go and went home for dinner with his wife. On Sunday morning, while the Roosevelts were at services in the East Room, the

Kennellys sat in a pew at St. Bonaventure and worshiped as they too infrequently had the opportunity to do.

Kennelly's mind, though, was not entirely engaged by the service. When he left the church, he telephoned Stan Szczygiel and gave him the name behind the license number. The Secret Service might be more likely than the DC police to have a file on that.

They did not, and Stan did something he distinctly disliked to do—he called the FBI. Saying the matter was of no great importance, he tried to keep the Federal Bureau from nibbing in. Meddling by the bungling, headline-hunting John Edgar Hoover was the last thing anyone needed in this investigation.

For all his faults, Hoover ran a tight ship. Within an hour of Szczygiel's call, a crisp young agent arrived at the White House with a manila envelope for him. It contained a report—

CONFIDENTIAL TO STANLISLAW SZCZYGIEL,
TREASURY DEPARTMENT, SECRET SERVICE
THE WHITE HOUSE

SUBJECT: VIRGINIA LICENSE 276 JBR

THE SUBJECT LICENSE PLATE WAS ISSUED ON JUNE 11, 1933 TO ONE ROBERT STRECKER AND HAS BEEN HELD BY HIM SINCE THAT DATE, BEING TRANSFERRED FROM ONE VEHICLE TO ANOTHER. IT IS CURRENTLY ASSIGNED TO A 1939 PACKARD SEDAN.

ROBERT STRECKER IS AN ATTORNEY AT LAW, ADMIT-

TED TO THE BAR IN VIRGINIA IN 1914 AND IN THE DISTRICT OF COLUMBIA IN 1915. HE IS 54 YEARS OF AGE, WIDOWED, AND THE FATHER OF A DAUGHTER, MARLENE STRECKER BAUM OF NEW YORK CITY.

HE IS ASSOCIATED WITH TWO LAW FIRMS, SUMMERS & STRECKER OF ALEXANDRIA, VIRGINIA, AND GRAND, DUGAN, LIPSCOMBE & STRECKER OF WASHINGTON.

MR. STRECKER'S NAME CAME TO THE ATTENTION OF THE BUREAU IN 1939, THROUGH THE FACT THAT HIS SON-IN-LAW, FREDERICK BAUM, WAS AN ACTIVE MEMBER OF THE GERMAN-AMERICAN BUND. MR. STRECKER HIMSELF IS A SUPPORTING MEMBER OF AMERICA-FIRST. HE HAS BEEN AFFILIATED WITH A NUMBER OF OTHER ORGANIZATIONS CONSIDERED BY THIS BUREAU LIKELY TO BE SEDITIOUS. HIS AFFILIATION WITH AND SUPPORT FOR THESE ORGANIZATIONS HAS CONTINUED SUBSEQUENT TO THE DECLARATIONS OF WAR BETWEEN THE UNITED STATES AND THE AXIS POWERS. HIS SUPPORT HAS BEEN CHIEFLY FINANCIAL, MR. STRECKER BEING A WEALTHY MAN BOTH BY INHERITANCE AND BY HIS SUCCESS IN THE PRACTICE OF LAW.

MR. STRECKER HAS BEEN OBSERVED VISITING OR IN THE COMPANY OF:

(1) MRS. FRANCES P. SCHROEDER, WIDOW OF JAMES L. SCHROEDER, WHO DIED IN ATLANTA PENITENTIARY IN OCTOBER 1942, HAVING SERVED ONLY THREE MONTHS OF A LIFE SENTENCE FOR TREASON, HAVING ASSISTED GERMAN SUBMARINE CREWS TO COME ASHORE ON AMERICAN

BEACHES AND TO ESTABLISH FALSE IDENTIFICATION DOCUMENTS IN THIS COUNTRY. IT WOULD APPEAR THAT MRS. SCHROEDER MAY BECOME THE SECOND MRS. STRECKER.

(2)MRS. ELIZABETH DILLING, PROMINENT NAZI SYMPATHIZER.

(3) DR. JOHN LAUDER, GRAND DRAGON OF THE KU KLUX KLAN OF VIRGINIA.

(4) SEVERAL INDIVIDUALS WHOSE IDENTITIES CANNOT BE DISCLOSED.

PLEASE ADVISE THIS BUREAU OF ANY ADDITIONAL INFORMATION IN YOUR POSSESSION.

Szczygiel shook his head. "I almost wish I hadn't asked," he muttered.

The First Lady made it a point never to go near the conference room when vital issues were under discussion. This morning, though, Winston Churchill specifically invited her to sit in for a while.

"You should know what kind of things occupy us," he said.

For this session Admiral King was not present. The President, the Prime Minister, and the generals were.

"We are going to have to say something significant to Uncle Joe Stalin," said the President. "He wants to know when we are going to open the Second Front."

"I am getting the same demand from our socialist friends," said the Prime Minister. "Low drew a cartoon about it. I am shown standing in front of a wall on which SECOND FRONT NOW! is rudely painted. I have stricken the word NOW and have substituted AT THE PROPER TIME."

"So far as I am concerned," said General Sir Alan Brooke, "we need not open a Second Front at all. Round-the-clock bombing will bring Germany to its knees. I know that our losses in men and machines are heavy, but they are as nothing compared to the losses we will experience if we attempt to send an army ashore on the coast of France. Our air strength is growing. It can destroy German industry, and without industry the Wehrmacht cannot fight."

"The problem with that is time," said the President. "Can we bring Hitler to his knees before his armies knock Russia out of the war?"

"I have to wonder," said General Eisenhower, "if we should continue to concentrate so much of our resources on Japan. We've got the Japs stopped. We can maintain the status quo in the Far East until we've settled the matter of Hitler."

"But consider," Churchill rumbled. "What if the Japanese attack through Burma and conquer *Inn-ja*? What then?"

Mrs. Roosevelt knew that the President was probably reflecting that the Prime Minister was thinking of the British Empire, which he was determined to preserve, even knowing that the President was by no means committed to any such goal.

"We have stopped the Japanese advance toward Australia," said Sir Alan. "Your great naval victories have stopped any advance they might want to make toward Hawaii or even California. But they still maintain major forces in China and Burma; and their naval forces in the South China Sea and the Bay of Bengal, which are not inconsiderable, have not been defeated. They entertain a fanciful dream: of advancing ever westward, across India, across Persia, and uniting with an eastward-advancing German force hurrying out of the Caucasus."

"Fanciful," said Marshall.

"But a horrible nightmare in the unlikely event that it should come to pass," said Churchill.

"I am not convinced it would be horrible, even if it happened," said Marshall. "The Japanese supply line would be so long and so thinly defended that we could cut it and leave their advanced divisions helpless."

"General MacArthur continues to warn us of impending enemy moves in his theater," said the President.

A moment's silence fell across the room as every one of the conferees suppressed the comments that came to their minds.

"I am still wondering what we can say to Uncle Joe," said the President.

"You can tell him this," said Marshall. "A cross-channel invasion cannot be mounted before the spring of 1944."

"And who will command?" asked Churchill. He fixed his eyes for a moment on General Sir Alan Brooke. "Since the vast majority of the troops under his command will be

Americans, I think we must agree that an American general should command."

"Certainly," said Sir Alan Brooke firmly—though he could not conceal his disappointment.

"I remember the name Schroeder," Mrs. Roosevelt said to Stan Szczygiel and Ed Kennelly as they sat in her study, over coffee, late that morning. "Of course I know who Mrs. Dilling is. I shall always be grateful to her for listing me in such distinguished company as Felix Frankfurter, H. L. Mencken, and Mahatma Gandhi—Communists all."

"You are known by the company you keep," said Szczygiel. "It would be better to be known by the company in which you are placed by kook list-makers."

"Schroeder," said Kennelly. "I believe it was three German spies that came ashore in Florida, from a submarine. He met them and gave them forged drivers' licenses, draft cards, Social Security cards, ration books, and assorted other paper: whatever junk a man might have in his pockets. He'd had all this stuff printed in a Washington print shop, where he'd paid a fortune for it. Unhappily for him, soldiers guarding the beach moved in on them and seized the spies along with their forged documents and Schroeder before they were a hundred yards away from the water."

"The Germans are still in Atlanta Penitentiary," said Mrs. Roosevelt. "Mr. Schroeder, who apparently could not face the prospect of life in prison, died of a heart attack not long after arriving there. At the time, a petition for a presidential pardon was on Franklin's desk. It bore the signatures of an odd variety of people. Mr. Schroeder would not have been pardoned. He might, though, have been given a commutation of sentence, to, say, five years."

"I see no reason why he should have had a commutation," said Szczygiel. "That kind—" He did not finish.

"I recall his wife saying she would not demean herself by making an appeal for clemency to President Roosevelt. Maybe someday when someone else was President, but never to '*that man.*' "

"Frances Schroeder," said Szczygiel. "She calls herself 'Frankie.' She's a striking figure. As was Schroeder. He was a member of Silver Shirts."

"Silver Shirts? What is that?" asked the First Lady.

"American Nazis," said Szczygiel. "And fervid anti-Semites. Some of the original American Nazis wore brown shirts, to identify themselves with Hitler's Brown Shirts, the Storm Troopers, the SA. Later on a man named Pelley formed what he considered an elite organization, modeled on Hitler's SS. They could have worn black shirts but instead Pelley chose silver, because the abbreviation for Silver Shirts would be SS. Weyrich, incidentally, had a copy of one of their pamphlets in his apartment—a vicious anti-Semitic tract, one of those that calls the President 'the Dutch Jew Rosenfeld.' "

Mrs. Roosevelt smiled wryly and shook her head. "We've heard that one many times."

"This business looks more and more like a botched attempt to assassinate the President," said Szczygiel.

"I should very much like to know," said Mrs. Roosevelt, "what was the purpose of an hour-long meeting between Mr. Weyrich's friends and the lawyer Mr. Strecker."

"It won't be easy to find out," said Ed Kennelly. "Strecker lives in Virginia. I can't get a warrant to search *his* place. I couldn't even if he lived in the District; we don't have anything on him."

"Where does Mrs. Schroeder live?" asked the First Lady.

"Georgetown," said Szczygiel. "Her late husband owned the Fashion Store."

"Really? I am familiar with it."

"It was the Schroeder Department Store until the sinking of the Lusitania in 1915, when anti-German sentiment in this country led Schroeder's father to change the name. Anyway, when he went to the penitentiary she took over the store. She owns and manages it now."

"A formidable woman," Kennelly added. "Well over six feet tall. As blonde as Harlow."

Mrs. Roosevelt laughed. "Tall women are formidable." She herself was more than six feet tall.

"It was not long after the death of her husband in the penitentiary," said Kennelly, "that she began to be seen out in society. She went to better bars than Eva Lee, but she became something of an habitué of the more elegant watering holes."

"Do we know anything more about the grand dragon—I mean, other than that he *is* the grand dragon?"

"Only that Mr. Strecker certainly chooses an odd circle of friends," said Szczygiel.

The Trident Conference continued during the afternoon, but the President suggested and the others agreed that they were entitled to relax on Sunday evening. General Marshall and Admiral King went home after sitting down for half an hour in the daily presidential cocktail party. The President liked to relax over movies. Bell & Howell had provided him a sixteen-millimeter sound projector, and several Hollywood studios sent sixteen-millimeter versions of their films to the White House. In years past, Missy LeHand had operated the projector and run films for the President in his bedroom, while they ate their dinners from trays sent up from the kitchen. Missy was in the hospital now, so the President had the projector and screen set up in the West Sitting Hall, and trays were brought up for all.

The President and the Prime Minister were there, with Generals Eisenhower and Brooke, plus Sarah Churchill and Kay Summersby. Mrs. Roosevelt didn't attend, but instead kept an appointment she had made to dine with the Morgenthaus: the Secretary of the Treasury and his wife, her long-time close friend Elinor.

The film was *Yankee Doodle Dandy,* starring James Cagney. The President was especially entertained by the brief scene in which *he* was portrayed meeting with George M. Cohan. Churchill didn't see that scene. By the time it came on the screen he was asleep.

X

WHEN JULIE LEFT HER boardinghouse on Monday morning, she found Ed Kennelly waiting in a Ford parked at the curb.

"I'll save you bus fare this morning," he said. "Hop in."

"Am I under arrest?"

"Not at all. I'll drive you to the White House."

Plainly she did not welcome a ride to the White House from Captain Edward Kennelly, DC Police, but she climbed into the car.

"Smoke?" he asked her, offering her his pack of Lucky Strikes.

She accepted a cigarette and a light. He lit one for himself before he started the car. A later generation of Americans would reject cigarettes as deadly and addictive, but in 1943 everyone smoked, and those who didn't were considered rather odd. Motion pictures portrayed wounded soldiers as gratefully accepting a last drag on a cigarette before they died. Bette Davis was known for her elegant way of handling a cigarette and smoking. So was Paul Henreid. Mrs. Roosevelt suspected that her husband, with his weakening heart, should not smoke. But she knew it would be useless to suggest to him that he stop it. That Louie Howe had died of his Sweet Caporals had not turned the President away from his Camels.

The morning was warm, and Julie was wearing a thin cotton dress: white with a pattern of blue and pink flowers. The outline of her bra was faintly visible.

"Well, have you retained a lawyer?" he asked her.

"No. Do I need a lawyer?"

"You've talked to one, anyway, haven't you?"

She shook her head. "I don't even know a lawyer. Of course, Paul was a lawyer, but—Do I *need* a lawyer?"

"You may if you don't stop lying to us."

"What have I lied about now!?" she asked irately.

"It may not be so much that you have lied as that you are withholding information. You know more about the death of Weyrich than you are telling us."

"Okay, copper," she sneered. "I'll 'fess up. I knocked Paul down with a candlestick and beat him to death with it. Then I stashed the gun on him. The way I got the gun into the White House was, I carried it in a crotch holster. Cops are too bashful to search a girl there."

"Julie . . ." said Kennelly, miming patience. "Weyrich wasn't beaten to death. He was killed with one hard blow to the back of his head—and not with a candlestick. And you couldn't have carried the gun in through the metal detectors."

"Which goes to show how much I know about how he got killed and who killed him."

"You say you loved him. Aren't you interested in helping us identify and bring to justice the man who killed him?"

"Of course," she said ruefully. "Of co-worse."

The First Lady dictated two "My Day" columns that morning. One of them had to do with a domestic problem that had become serious. Inconceivable though it might be to the average American, the nation's defense industry was suffering an acute shortage of animal fats. Kitchen fats, the viscous fluids housewives poured out of skillets, were an essential resource. These fats contained glycerine, and glycerine was a necessary ingredient of smokeless gunpowder, plus certain medicines. Even though people knew this, they were not saving their fats and turning them in for processing. The government had run newspaper ads and distributed leaflets, imploring people to save their fats.

A pound of kitchen fat, about to be poured out with the garbage, would produce enough glycerine to manufacture a pound and a quarter of gunpowder. It was estimated that a billion pounds of kitchen fat was discarded every year. She called that a billion and a quarter pounds of powder American boys fighting overseas would not have.

She would not know for months if her column had any impact. She wrote it and hoped.

Ed Kennelly arrived. Stan Szczygiel, too, came to Mrs. Roosevelt's second-floor study.

"She's lied again," said Kennelly. "She says she doesn't know any lawyers, but she was with Strecker for an hour in Pipe's apartment, after which he drove her home."

"Is it conceivable she doesn't know Mr. Strecker is a lawyer?" asked Mrs. Roosevelt.

"It might be conceivable—except for just one little thing. Strecker called me half an hour ago and advised me he was Miss Finch's lawyer and that I was not to interrogate her any further outside his presence. He's full of you-know-what."

"Did you tell him so?" asked Szczygiel.

Kennelly shrugged. "Why educate him? I'm sure he knows what I can and can't do and that I don't need any guff from him, but I just told him I would make a note in the file that he was her lawyer, and—" Kennelly grinned. "And I would give him a call if I had her in jail again."

"It should not," said Mrs. Roosevelt, "bolster a case against a suspect when she engages an attorney, but I am afraid it does."

"It might not if it weren't Strecker," said Kennelly. "The connection is just too suggestive."

"I should like to have the answer to a question," said the First Lady. "What is the significance of Mr. Strecker's acquaintance with the Grand Dragon of the Klu Klux Klan? And . . . was Miss Finch by any chance a member of the KKK in Tennessee?"

"I believe you have better resources to answer those questions than I have," said Kennelly.

In fact, she did. She phoned the office of the Anti-Defamation League of B'Nai Brith. She told a representative what her questions were, and he said he would be glad to come to the White House before the end of the afternoon to give her the results of a little research he would have to do. Then she called Congressman Warren Mellon.

"It is a pleasure, ma'am. A singular pleasure to talk with you any time."

"I have a question for you, Congressman. In fact, two or three questions."

"Any questions at all, ma'am."

"Well, sir. To start with, is the Ku Klux Klan still active in your part of Tennessee?"

Mellon was silent for a moment. "I suppose I have to say it is, Mrs. Roosevelt. Nothin' like it once was. You recall that Senator Black, being from Alabama, confessed after the President nominated him for the Supreme Court that he had been, briefly, a member of the Klan. A young man couldn't hope to succeed in the practice of law or win election to any kind of office who was not a member of the Klan. So, even Mr. Justice Hugo Black was a member, once. And so was I, ma'am, so was I."

"I understand," she said.

"In my part of Tennessee, bein' a member of the Klan was like bein' a member of Rotary. It was a social club. I swear to you, Mrs. Roosevelt—we never burnt crosses or beat or lynched anybody, or even intimidated anybody. White robes and masks . . . I never owned any, much less ever wore any. There's Klan and there's Klan, you see."

"I quite understand, Congressman Mellon."

"Anyway . . . ?"

"Well, I was curious to know if Julie was affiliated with the women's branch of the Ku Klux Klan."

"Not that I ever heard of."

"So she was not anti-Negro, anti-Semitic, anti-Catholic . . . ?"

"I never said that. What Julie was—and frankly is—is what we in the South call 'poor white trash.' I guess I told you that before. One of the things about them is, they always figure somebody else is getting what they're entitled to. Money . . . Jobs . . . They kind of hate anybody that gets ahead of 'em. I never heard Julie talk much in a political way, but I can tell you that she always figured other folks got things she was entitled to."

"Because she was pure white," Mrs. Roosevelt suggested.

"Like you and me, ma'am. She figured she was as good as any of us. And she resented it—as her daddy resented it—that she didn't get what she figured was her share."

"Bitter?"

"Let me put it this way. You remember how Mark Twain wrote in *Huckleberry Finn* about how his 'pap' figured he was a white man, which made him superior to anybody who wasn't as white as he was? Julie's father talked that way. I can't say if she bought it. But she was sure exposed to it."

"Would you say she hated Negroes?"

"I wouldn't say she hated them. But she figured she was better than them and always would be, no matter what; she was *born* better than them. If a Negro made more money than her daddy made, he resented it; and *she* resented it. I'm sure she never did anything bad about it. It just burned inside her."

"Burned with resentment . . ."

"Oh, yes. Now that I think of it, that time when she was in jail a Negro woman was in there, too. Julie didn't like that at all. She and that Negro woman had to use the same toilet, wash their faces in the same basin. I guess a lot of folks were uncomfortable about that, but the county couldn't afford to build a separate jail, so that's the way it was. She fumed about it. She wasn't as unhappy about being in jail as she was being locked in a cage with a Negro."

"You have been most helpful, Congressman."

The representative from the Anti-Defamation League arrived about 4:30 P.M. He was a Jew, wearing a yarmulke: a man in his fifties, as Mrs. Roosevelt judged, with little left of his gray hair. His dark eyes were sharp, shifting, and alert. He had a Roman nose. When light struck him from one angle, a white stubble of whiskers caught it and gleamed faintly. Apparently he had shaved very early that morning and, if his whiskers had been dark they would be appearing as a five-o'clock shadow.

"My name is Benjamin Goldish," he said as he sat down in the chair the First Lady had indicated to him.

"I am pleased to meet you, Mr. Goldish. It is most kind of you to come."

Goldish opened a small briefcase. "As I suspected we would, we have a file on Dr. John Lauder. I telephoned our B'Nai Brith chapter in Richmond for confirmation and the latest information. Here is a copy of our summary sheet on him."

He handed Mrs. Roosevelt a photostat—

Subject: Dr. John Lauder, Richmond, Virginia; Grand Dragon of the Ku Klux Klan of Virginia.

Dr. Lauder is a physician and surgeon, a graduate of Emory University and the medical school of the University of Virginia. He is 55 years of age and has practiced medicine for 24 years. He served in the army in World War I, with the rank of lieutenant, then of captain. He is an active member of the American Legion. He was married in 1919 and is the father of two sons, both of whom are serving in the army. He and his family live in a home that has been in the Lauder family since 1834. He has never occupied any other residence.

Dr. Lauder joined the Ku Klux Klan in 1921 and has been an active member ever since, holding various offices in the organization. He travels extensively on Klan business and attends meetings throughout the South.

Before Pearl Harbor he was active in America-First and traveled to its meetings in Washington, Baltimore, Philadelphia, and New York.

Dr. Lauder is a bitter and outspoken anti-Semite. He sought to exclude Jews from the American Legion and the Richmond Chamber of Commerce. He headed a committee to discharge Negro women from jobs as domestics in Richmond, "to put them in their place and discourage them from getting uppity ideas."

He chaired another committee to prevent Negroes from becoming members of labor unions. "They wouldn't want to anyway," he said, "if it wasn't for kike agitators stirring them up." He characterizes union organizers and recruiters as "kike Reds" and calls on Klan members to identify them and run them out of the South.

"This is a serious indictment," said Mrs. Roosevelt, tapping the sheets with a finger.

"There is much more," said Goldish. "That is only our summary. Every statement in there is supported by documentation: newspaper stories, letters, transcriptions of speeches, and so on."

"It is frightening to know there are such people in our country."

He nodded. "But there are," he said solemnly.

"Yes," she agreed.

"Now . . . You said Dr. Lauder seemed to be a friend of Mr. Robert Strecker. We have a dossier on Mr. Strecker, too. It is not nearly so frightening as what we have on Dr. Lauder, but it says in essence that Attorney Strecker has constantly identified himself with anti-Semitic and racist individuals and organizations. Unfortunately, in this respect, Attorney Strecker's daughter married an active member of and spokesman for the German-American Bund."

"Frederick Baum," she said.

"He was drafted in May of 1942. He speaks fluent German, and Mr. Strecker lobbied for him to be commissioned in Army Intelligence. With his background, the army would not trust him; so today he remains a private first class and is a guard at a prisoner of war camp in Texas. He is likely to stay right there and at that rank for the remainder of the war. Mr. Strecker is quite bitter about it. I have a letter he wrote to Congressman Martin Dies." Goldish smiled shyly. "Please don't ask how we happen to have this in our possession."

The letter read—

Dear Congressman Dies,
You will, I hope, remember me. I introduced you to the American Legion Convention in Baltimore in 1940, commending you on your excellent work as chairman of the House Committee on Un-American Activities.

Sir, I do not believe I exaggerate when I characterize my son-in-law, PFC Frederick Baum, as a political prisoner of the Roosevelt Administration. The young man speaks fluent, idiomatic German, is a skilled Alpinist, and when he was inducted into the army last year I suggested he would make an excellent intelligence officer. Instead, he was dispatched to a POW camp in your district in Texas to serve in no better a capacity than as a guard outside the wire. This is his punishment for having opposed U.S. involvement in the war in Europe.

I need hardly tell you, Congressman, that this current administration is arbitrary, vindictive, and altogether vicious in dealing with those who dare to disagree with the temporary—let us hope very temporary—President of the United States.

Since my son-in-law is stationed in

```
your district, I venture to ask your
assistance in correcting this injustice.
```

"The man is bitter," remarked Mrs. Roosevelt.

"The nature of the relationship between Mr. Strecker and Dr. Lauder—" Goldish shrugged "—is not known to us."

"Have you any information on Mr. Weyrich?"

"No, none."

"Well, I . . . I am most grateful to you."

"May I then ask a favor of you?"

"Of course."

Goldish drew a deep breath. "Mrs. Roosevelt, there are certain facts of which I hope you are aware. The Nazis are rounding up Jews by the tens of thousands in Poland and Russia and summarily putting them to death. They make no pretense anymore that arrested Jews are criminals or 'enemies of the state.' They herd them into camps simply because they are Jews and methodically murder them. Hundreds of thousands work as slaves, but other hundreds of thousands do not have even that sorry option; they are simply shot or asphyxiated. I cannot believe the President is not aware of this."

"He *is* aware of it, to a degree," said Mrs. Roosevelt. "Mr. Goldish, I will tell you a very deep secret. Some weeks ago intelligence sources identified a prison camp in Poland as one in which thousands of prisoners were being gassed to death and their bodies cremated. It was suggested that we bomb that camp out of existence. There were three problems. The first was that the camp is beyond the range of our bombers. The second was that such a raid would inevitably kill many, many prisoners. The third problem was that the Nazis would simply rebuild the camp or build another one, so we would have achieved little."

Goldish nodded. "Or worse than little."

"There has been talk of destroying railroad bridges between, say, Warsaw and the camps. But—"

"I know," said Goldish sadly. "Hundreds of bridges. And always new camps."

"The only real solution is to win the war," said the First Lady.

"And terminate Naziism once and for all. But in the meantime my people are bleeding—bleeding and suffocating and starving."

"The President will do everything he can."

XI

"STAN," SAID MRS. ROOSEVELT to Szczygiel. "Look at these several letters, would you? I should appreciate your looking at them from the standpoint that every typewriter leaves its fingerprints, so to speak. That is to say, every typewriter has one or more ill-formed or damaged letters, no typewriter aligns its letters with absolute precision, and so on. I have been studying the several letters Mr. Weyrich wrote to Julie asking her for a date and so on, then the farewell letter he wrote her. Do you see the distinction?"

Szczygiel squinted at the letters. He looked up and smiled. "I . . . Do you have something in mind. Why don't you relieve an old man's eyesight and tell me what you see?"

She smiled at Szczygiel's reference to being an old man. His alertness of mind belied the years on his calendar. In any event, she was not willing to concede that a man only fourteen years her senior was "an old man."

"Notice the letter 'u,' " she said. "It is out of alignment.

It is too high in his letters asking for dates and proclaiming his love. But in the letter when he told her he might not see her for a long time, it was correctly aligned. The typewriter's signature is correct in other respects. The letter 'g' has a gap in the tail, the letter 'i' has only a faint dot. And so on. It suggests that—Well . . . is this fanciful? It suggests that the typewriter was repaired between the date of the love letters and the date of the farewell letter—and that a technician corrected the misalignment of the 'u.' "

"Which means what, ma'am?"

"*I* have surmised—I don't know if you have—that Mr. Weyrich left his office last Tuesday night expecting never to return. If so, why would he have had his typewriter repaired a few days before?"

"Let me look into that, ma'am."

The First Lady had not intended to be present at a reception that evening, being given by the Daughters of the American Revolution in honor of General Douglas MacArthur. Her disagreement with the Daughters over the Marian Anderson concert was well known. (The DAR had refused to allow the supremely talented American contralto to appear at their Constitution Hall because she was a Negro.) A concert was therefore held at the Lincoln Memorial, where it was attended by many thousands of people of all races. The DAR had come out with egg on its face. It had become a joke in newspapers everywhere except in the Deep South. Nonetheless, the Daughters continued to send the First Lady invitations, pro forma, doubtless not expecting she would attend.

She would not have attended except that she saw on the list of sponsors a name that interested her. Frances P. Schroeder, the wife of the man who had died in Atlanta Penitentiary while serving a life sentence for treason, the now owner and manager of The Fashion Store, and possible fiancée of Robert Strecker.

The reception was held in the foyer of Constitution Hall. Punch and cookies were served, and there were to be several speeches. When she was greeted by the officers, Mrs. Roosevelt told them that she was happy to be there but might not be able to stay very long. She would like, she said, to circulate and greet the guests.

Identifying Frances Schroeder was no problem. She was the only woman in the room who was taller than the First Lady. And she was, as Ed Kennelly had put it, as blond as Harlow. Indeed, her dark eyebrows made it apparent that her hair, like Harlow's, had been stripped. It was coiffed into a shiny, wavy, close-fitting cap, leaving her earlobes exposed so as to display her dangling diamond earrings. A matching necklace hung in her cleavage. Her white silk dress was interwoven with glittering spangles. To Mrs. Roosevelt she was not so much reminiscent of the late Jean Harlow as she was of Mae West.

As she crossed the room, the First Lady was the center of attention, not all of it favorable. The DAR officers led women to her to be introduced. The crowd included many who did not forgive her for her stand on Marian Anderson. To others she was simply the outspoken, aggressive wife of "that man." They managed to extend elementary courtesy, just the same—until one of the women presented Frances Schroeder.

Mrs. Schroeder did not extend her hand. For a brief moment she turned away from the woman with whom she was talking, nodded curtly, and said, "Hello, Mrs. Roosevelt." With that she turned back to her friend and resumed their conversation.

The buxom, white-haired officer of the DAR blushed visibly. "I am sorry," she said. "You see, Mrs. Schroeder blames the President for the death of her husband."

"I am not quite sure what she thinks the President could have done."

"Kept us out of the war. Her husband, you see, was of German ancestry and of complete German sympathies. He was outraged by such things as Lend Lease, which he said absolutely *compelled* Hitler to declare war on the United States after the Japanese attack on Pearl Harbor. And I am afraid Mrs. Schroeder shares her husband's opinions. I do apologize for her rudeness."

"Please. You need not apologize. Or be embarrassed. It was a minor rudeness compared to some mail I receive—or some editorials and columns I read."

"Oh, dear!"

"It is widely and sincerely believed in some parts of the country that I have for some time been involved in a meretricious relationship with a Negro sharecropper, whom I am supposed to have met during one of my tours of the poverty-stricken areas of the South. It would sicken you to read some of the suggestions made against me. I cannot even repeat them, they are so vile."

Stan Szczygiel sat at a desk in the White House accounting office and worked his way through a file of bills and receipts. He wondered if Weyrich's typewriter had gone out for repair or if there were some other explanation as to why the "u" that had been misaligned was suddenly aligned when he typed the farewell letter. It was not inconceivable that a typist, annoyed by a misaligned letter, had used his fingers to bend the type bar slightly. He himself had sometimes tried to do it, usually with bad results. So had the office of the special counsel to the President sent his typewriter out for repair within the month before his death?

He had. The bill was dated April 23, 1943—

LINCOLN OFFICE MACHINES
To cleaning, lubricating, and
realigning characters on Underwood
typewriter—$14.50

There was more. Julie's Underwood had gone out *twice* in April, also to Lincoln Office Machines: once for cleaning and lubricating, once to replace a broken type bar.

Three typewriter repair jobs in the month preceding

Weyrich's death? Szczygiel decided this demanded investigation.

Ed Kennelly found Eva at the Ben Butler Bar, where he had seen her before, where he expected to see her tonight. He had done a little checking and knew that Rusty Pipe would not be appearing much before midnight. The engineers were surveying and blocking a nineteenth century drainage tunnel between Union Station and a main interceptor drainage tunnel half a mile away. Rainwater had not run through the old tunnel in more than fifty years, but it was a place where bombs could be detonated with devastating damage to several facilities.

Habitués of the BB were chary of Captain Kennelly. They knew him as a cop and a tough man. The knot around Eva at the bar broke when he approached.

"Get me another drink of that single-malt Scotch," she said, "and I'll tell you anything."

He was surprised. Eva was not entirely sober. She was wearing a simple white cotton blouse and a black skirt a bit shorter than most seen in Washington in 1943.

When they were sitting at a table he asked conversationally where Rusty was—though of course he knew exactly where Rusty was.

"Why should I know where he is?" she asked.

"Well . . . your relationship with him is a little more intimate than you led me to believe."

"What makes you think so?"

"Hey, kid, I'm a cop! It's my business to know things—like that you were in bed with him Saturday afternoon."

"Sat—Jesus Christ!"

"You can deny it if you want to."

"Since I talked to you last week, some guys have told me about you. Guys . . . guys here in the BB. From the way I get it, you wouldn't say what you just said if you didn't *know*. What I can't figure is, *how* do you know? You hidin' in the closet?"

"What *I* can't figure," said Kennelly, "is why you would insist a guy is a creep, then crawl between the sheets with him."

"He's been nice to me," said Eva.

"He got to see you naked, finally."

"C'mon, Kennelly!"

"Alright. Is he a creep, or isn't he a creep?"

Eva glanced around the room. "Okay," she said. "Look at that." She showed him a solitaire diamond set in a white-gold ring. She wore it on the middle finger of her left hand.

"Meaning?" he asked.

"Well . . . The guy is more lonely than anything else. I mean, he's a long way from home and—"

"Who's Strecker, Eva?"

"Jesus! Is there anything you don't know?"

"Eva . . . As it stands right now, you're in no trouble—yet. Julie is. For one reason. She lies."

"You have to feel sorry for Julie. You really do. She was in love with Paul."

Kennelly fell silent and waited as two beers and two Scotches were put in front of them.

"When she came home after spending a night in jail, did she say it was the only time she was ever in jail?"

"Yeah. She said it was awful. It was scary," said Eva, tossing back her Scotch.

"Well, it was the *fourth* time she'd been in jail. She was in jail on three separate occasions back in Tennessee, once for fifteen days, for shoplifting."

"So?"

"So, the truth is not in her, Eva. Don't let her get *you* involved in something."

"Like what?"

"What do you suppose? What's your guess? Why is Paul Weyrich dead?"

"You're talkin' about *murder?* You're talking about me being some way involved in the murder of Paul Weyrich?"

"Don't *get* involved, Eva. That's what I'm saying—don't *get* involved."

"You're saying that Julie and Rusty and Mr. Strecker are some way involved in—"

"I'm saying we're trying to find out."

"Well . . . what could *I* know?"

"Saturday afternoon, Julie and Rusty and Strecker met at Rusty's apartment. Why were *you* there?"

"I don't know, exactly. Rusty'd asked me to come. We were going to do something else, like I guess you know."

"You were there an hour before Julie and Strecker left. What did they talk about all that time?"

"Nothin' much. We had some drinks. There was a lot of political talk."

"Like what?"

"Well . . . Let's see. They talked about why Winston Churchill is at the White House. President Roosevelt's scared, Mr. Strecker said. He's looking for a great man like Mr. Churchill to back him up, give him a better reputation."

Kennelly stiffened as he filled with breath. "Churchill," he said dourly. "You think he's in Washington?"

"They talked about it."

"Was that the first you ever heard of it?"

Eva nodded. "Is it a big deal?"

"It's a national-defense secret. Whoever reveals it can go to the penitentiary, big time. Julie knew about it, from working for Weyrich. If she told Strecker and Rusty, not to mention you, she could go to Alderson for years and years and years."

"Alderson?"

"The federal reformatory for women, in West Virginia."

Eva's eyes widened. "I haven't told anybody!"

"But Strecker and Rusty already knew it."

"Which doesn't mean Julie told them. She didn't tell me. I just figured it out from what I heard them say."

"*They talked in front of you?* Eva! They wouldn't just casually drop it in front of you that they were in possession of that kind of secret. Look. The Secret Service can arrest you—and the others, too—and hold you at least until Churchill goes back to London. You won't be in the DC jail where Julie was. You'll be in a military or naval facility, where you can't get word out."

Almost surreptitiously, yet not surreptitiously at all, Kennelly exchanged her empty glass for his glass of Scotch. They said nothing, but she drank it immediately.

"S'pose," she suggested, "I denied I ever said this to you. I mean, s'pose I say I never mentioned Churchill to you."

"In peacetime that might be good enough—your word against mine—but this is wartime, the nation's survival is at stake, and standards are different. I've got no reason to lie. You do—or you may have."

Eva blinked, forcing back tears from her eyes. "I never met Mr. Strecker before Saturday. He's a scary man. Rusty's afraid of him. He just looks at you and, I mean, you figure he's thinkin', 'I'd just as soon kill you as look at you.' They needed somethin' from me."

"Needed what?"

"They wanted to write somethin' they called a manifesto. They wanted it typed on a typewriter that couldn't possibly be traced to any of them—like my secretarial typewriter at the Archives. Julie had been after me for some time to type this thing for them. I said I would. I don't know what a manifesto is—what *this* manifesto is, anyway. I guess they figured they could trust me, after I agreed to type their manifesto. Anyway, they didn't say much in front of me, only that they wouldn't need the manifesto right now but I should remember I'd agreed to type it."

"And Rusty gave you the diamond ring . . . ?"

"That afternoon. He was an *angel!*"

"On Saturday afternoon they trusted you with important secrets, and Rusty gave you a diamond ring. Interesting afternoon," said Kennelly.

Eva ran her hands over her eyes, and her fingers came away wet with tears. "What you gonna do, lock me up?"

"God forbid," said Kennelly solemnly.

"I never *have been*. Julie may have been, but I never was. The idea *scares* me!"

"You've been scared for some time," said Kennelly.

"I want out of Washington! I want to go home!"

"Home to . . . ?"

"I'm sorry I ever came to this town! Captain Kennelly!" She put her tear-wet hands on his. "Captain Kennelly! I'm a faithful Catholic—at least, I try to be. I've confessed everything to Father Francis Grogan at St. Bartholomew's. He says I've got myself involved in something very wrong."

"Tell me what."

"I don't *know* what! I'm just a good-time girl. These people—Julie and Rusty and Strecker—are way beyond me! So was Paul."

"They wanted something more from you than that you type a manifesto. What was it?"

Eva sighed. "Julie wanted me to swear that when I got home the night Paul died, she was there in our room, in bed. Whether she was or wasn't."

"And?"

"She was there alright. Crying her eyes out. And she wouldn't say why."

XII

FROM THE DAY WHEN the Trident Conference first assembled, it was understood that it would not end in one week, or even two. The issues to be decided were too monumental to be decided in a few days.

They had already decided that Stalin was to be advised that the opening of the Second Front—that is the Allied invasion of northwestern Europe would begin in May of the following year, not before. It was simply not possible to mount a cross-Channel invasion before then—and indeed that was pressing hard and would involve major risk. The President continued to entertain a suspicion that Churchill did not care much if the Soviet Union fell, even to Hitler. In his philosophy, Communism was as bad as Naziism and maybe even worse. So . . . no invasion until the Allies were ready. In the meantime the United States and Britain would subject the Reich to round-the-clock bombing.

Churchill told the conferees that Göring had said if

any enemy bomber ever reached Berlin, the German people could call him "Meyer"—which was what the German people now called him.

They had agreed that the supreme commander for the operation to which they had given the name Overlord would be an American, presumably Marshall.

They agreed to support both of two plans for the Pacific—that MacArthur would continue his island-hopping campaign in the south and Nimitz would seize base after base island in the north.

To be decided: What to do about German submarine activities in the North Atlantic? How to get more supplies through to the Soviet Union? How seriously to take Chiang Kai-shek?

Madame Chiang was a Christian, educated in the United States, and she had a formidable following in Congress and among the American people, who were dismally naive about China. American missionaries returning from China had constantly assured the American people that only the warlords and the Japanese stood in the way of China becoming a Christian nation. Few understood that Generalissimo Chiang was himself nothing but a warlord who tolerated his wife's Christianity as a useful propaganda device. What was worse, he had almost no army at his command, none that is, in which he could place trust. To the Chinese, Chiang Kai-shek was anything but a revered leader. The President knew this. Mrs. Roosevelt knew it. Churchill knew it. The question was, how could this little warlord, referred to as "Peanut" by General Still-well, be of use in the great war in the Pacific?

Above all, what risks to take with Enigma? That the code-breakers at Bletchley Park had deciphered the Reich's most sophisticated code was the greatest secret of the war. Churchill had allowed Coventry to be bombed rather than send up RAF fighters and reveal that he had known the German bombers were coming. The British navy knew where Nazi submarine wolf packs were prowling, but to attack and destroy them would betray that the Enigma code had been broken. What was important enough to reveal that?

The conferees knew Enigma had been broken. Roosevelt, Churchill, Brooke, Marshall, Leahy . . . Very few other men in the world knew. It was only during this conference that the secret was divulged to General Eisenhower. MacArthur didn't know. Nimitz didn't know. Montgomery didn't know. Mountbatten didn't know.

Anyone who discovered that secret without authorization would have been locked up incommunicado until the war was over.

Mrs. Roosevelt didn't know.

Stan Szczygiel appeared at Lincoln Office Machines when it opened. He went in and showed his badge to the severe-looking young woman behind the counter.

"Yes, sir. Mr. Benedict will be with you in a moment."

Alonzo Benedict was a small man who had the very

air of one who could work with the complexities of small machines, with dexterous fingers, and penetrating eyes. Szczygiel's impression was that he was maybe sixty years old.

"The White House," he said. "Yes, we do service typewriters from the White House. Not all the typewriters there. Some of them. We have no contract. But sometimes they call us and ask us to pick up a machine. It's because we're convenient, I suppose."

Szczygiel handed over three invoices. "You did these jobs?" he asked.

"Yes. Of course. That's our billing form. Yes, we did this repair work."

"You picked these up and returned them?"

"As a matter of fact, no," said Benedict, running his right hand over his liver-spotted bald head. "Mr. Weyrich—I have heard since, unfortunately, that he is deceased—brought these typewriters in and picked them up himself."

"Why?"

"He said he was in a very great hurry for them."

"Was there anything odd about these typewriters?"

"No, sir. Perfectly ordinary Underwood and Remington. Somewhat antiquated. I am compelled to tell you, sir, that equipment from the White House tends to be old and worn. Money should be made available to buy such an important office better machines."

"I agree. But why did the Underwood come in twice within the same week?"

"Mr. Weyrich dropped it and bent a shaft that runs through the undercarriage."

"What do you take to be the significance of that, Stan?" the First Lady asked Szczygiel.

"I have a feeling that your thoughts and mine may be running in the same direction," said Szczygiel.

Mrs. Roosevelt nodded, picked up the telephone, and told the White House operator to get her Captain Kennelly at DC police headquarters. When Kennelly came on the line, she asked him, "Ed, where is the Colt automatic that was found on the body of Mr. Weyrich?"

"It's in a locker here at headquarters."

"Could you bring it here?"

"I can if they'll let me in with it."

"I'll see to that. Could you come now?"

"I'll be there directly."

She telephoned the colonel in command of the military detail guarding the White House and asked him to see to it that Captain Kennelly was allowed to enter with an unloaded .32 caliber Colt automatic. Then she called the usher's office and asked that the two typewriters be brought to her study.

Two more people than she wanted assembled half an hour later. The colonel had insisted that an army lieutenant and a sergeant accompany Kennelly while he was carrying a pistol in the White House.

"I assume, Lieutenant Dugan, that since you are

assigned here, you are accustomed to witnessing confidential matters."

"Absolutely, ma'am," said the lieutenant.

"Very well. What you are about to see and hear is highly confidential and must not be revealed to anyone. Now . . . Ed. The automatic."

Kennelly was carrying the Colt in a heavy manila envelope. He took it out.

"I assume it comes apart," said Mrs. Roosevelt. "Does that require tools?"

"No, ma'am," said the sergeant. "That weapon can be field-stripped very easy. I can do it. Until the Colt forty-five was picked to replace it, this was the standard army officer's sidearm. Anyway, it field-strips just about the same way as the forty-five. You want me to do it?"

"Please," said Mrs. Roosevelt.

The sergeant pulled out the empty magazine. He pulled back the slide and examined the chamber, to be sure there was not a round in it. Then he dry-fired the pistol at the floor. He pulled back the slide again and pushed up the safety lever. This locked the slide open and left the barrel exposed. He twisted the barrel and pulled it out. With the barrel out, the slide slipped off the frame, and the recoil spring fell out.

All this took about twenty seconds and left five separate parts: the slide, the frame, the barrel, the recoil spring, and the magazine.

"Thank you very much, Sergeant," said the First Lady.

"Now let's turn these typewriters upside down. Obviously the assembled pistol could not be hidden inside one of them, but maybe the parts will fit in."

The largest individual part was the frame, which included the grip and trigger with the trigger guard. It would not fit inside the Remington, but with some pushing it would fit in the Underwood—provided one slightly bent a shaft that ran from side to side.

With that part inside the Underwood, the slide fit up inside the Remington. The barrel, the magazine, and the spring were easy fits. Residue of tape could be seen on parts inside both typewriters.

"A steel pistol fit inside two steel typewriters," said Mrs. Roosevelt. "That would defeat your metal detectors, wouldn't it, Lieutenant Dugan?"

"It sure would, ma'am. The detector wouldn't know one piece of steel from another."

"Which suggests an addition to your routine search procedures, doesn't it?"

"Yes, it does. I'll give the word to the colonel."

"One more question. Where *is* the metal detector?"

"There are two, ma'am," said the Lieutenant Dugan. "One is in the door to the south entry on the ground floor, and one is in the north portico on the first floor: the state entrances to the White House. Anyone who enters through any other door must submit to a personal search."

"*I've* never been searched."

The Lieutenant smiled broadly. "No, ma'am, and neither has the President."

"I believe we have solved one element of the mystery. Mr. Weyrich carried the pistol into the White House, probably through the South Portico, then through the ground-floor hall to the West Wing. He carried it right through the metal detector."

"Worse than that," said the lieutenant. "One of our fellows probably carried it for him: took it out of the trunk of his car and—"

"As a courtesy," said Stan Szczygiel.

"Which solves one element of the mystery. Sergeant, will you reassemble the pistol for us?"

When the lieutenant and sergeant were gone, Mrs. Roosevelt spoke to Ed and Stan. "Field-stripping the pistol took a good deal of handling. I doubt there are any fingerprints on it except those of the sergeant."

"We checked for fingerprints last week," said Kennelly. "It had been wiped clean."

"Why would Mr. Weyrich have wiped his fingerprints off a pistol he was carrying? Also, did you check for fingerprints on the inside parts, such as the barrel?"

"No," said Ed. "I'll order a check—assuming the sergeant left us any. Of course, we can't blame him . . ."

"We've assumed something," said Stan Szczygiel. "We've assumed Weyrich planted the pistol parts in the typewriters. Isn't it possible that someone else put them in the typewriters?"

"Who?" asked Kennelly.

"Julie," said Stan. "She'd have needed the cooperation of someone at Lincoln Office Machines. Benedict could have been lying. He could have picked up and delivered the typewriters. I've circulated this memo to the security staff—

MEMORANDUM

From: Stanlislaw Szczygiel, Special Agent, United States Secret Service

To: All personnel, Army, Secret Service, and White House Police engaged in guarding the White House

Anyone who observed the late Paul Weyrich carrying typewriters into or out of the WH will contact me immediately. The incident, if it occurred, would have occurred late in April or early in May.

Please advise me also of any other deliveries of typewriters you observed during the period.

"I learned last night," said Kennelly, "that Julie wanted an alibi for the night when Weyrich was killed. She had asked Eva to swear she was home in bed when Eva came home. In fact, she was, and Eva never needed to lie about it."

"Would she have, if needed?" asked Szczygiel.

"I don't know. Probably. Major Pipe gave her a diamond ring Saturday afternoon. It was a reward for something more than just going to bed with him."

Mrs. Roosevelt leaned back in her chair, closed her eyes, and shook her head. "We have learned a bit," she said. "We know that Julie Finch and, we must suppose, Mr. Weyrich were involved with a group of people who hate the President. We know some are lying to us. We know how the gun got in. We've made no progress, though, toward learning who killed Mr. Weyrich and why."

"Information is information," said Kennelly. "Sooner or later it begins to fit together."

"Well, let me throw out another bit of speculation. Whoever killed Mr. Weyrich has access to the White House. He was *in* the house. He knew something of the way the guards work. He killed Mr. Weyrich and made his way out."

"Maybe Rusty Pipe knows another tunnel," said Szczygiel.

"It might not require a tunnel," said Mrs. Roosevelt. "It could be a conduit or a duct, anything a man could crawl through."

"Pipe would know, if anyone would," said Kennelly.

"The other possibility," said Szczygiel, "is that the killer is a member of the staff."

"Someone who is in the White House constantly," said the First Lady.

"And someone, therefore, who is a continuing threat."

• • •

At 12:30 P.M. Mrs. Roosevelt kept an appointment for lunch with Mary McLeod Bethune, a presidential adviser on Negro affairs. Mrs. Bethune had also been Director of Negro Affairs, National Youth Administration. She had a reputation as a respected educator.

"I am sure," she said, "that you and the President have burdens to bear that are more pressing than any of *my* concerns."

"In the long run, Mary, no concern of mine, nor of the President's, is more important than achieving racial justice in our country."

"It is such a tragedy, though," said Mrs. Bethune, "when a young man entirely competent to, say, fly a fighter plane is assigned to be a mess boy. It's bad for that boy. It's bad for the country."

"I entirely agree. The Tuskegee airmen—"

"Prove the point," said Mrs. Bethune. "Crispus Attucks was killed in the Boston Massacre. Negro regiments fought heroically in the Civil War. But even today when a Negro recruit shows up, some officer assumes he is only fit to shovel manure."

"Shovel shit," said Mrs. Roosevelt.

Mrs. Bethune nodded crisply and smiled faintly. "Shovel that. Some places, Negro boys with passes don't dare go into town for a beer."

"I know. I assure you the President knows."

"Well . . . I don't disagree with the President's priorities. The first thing we have to do is win this war. At least my people aren't being herded into murder camps and put to death by the hundreds of thousands."

"Mary . . . Do you believe that is happening?"

"I haven't the least doubt of it. So Negroes may have to continue their suffering while this war is being won. But after—"

"After . . ." said the First Lady. "I promise you we will do everything we can to bring justice."

"We have every confidence in you, Mrs. Roosevelt."

When Major Ross Pipe arrived at his apartment, about six, he was surprised to find himself confronted by Captain Edward Kennelly, District Police, who had been waiting in a car and joined him on the porch of his building.

"I guess it's an honor," he said to Kennelly. "To what do I owe it?"

"Just like to talk with you a little."

"Well, you don't say no to the police. Inside?"

"Sure."

Kennelly did not suggest to Pipe that he had been inside this apartment before.

"Hey . . . uh . . . When you work where I work all day, the first thing you want to do when you get home is take a shower. Would you mind if I do that? Five minutes? While you have a drink?"

"Deal," said Kennelly.

"Bar's in the kitchen. Whatever you want. I'll be as quick as possible."

Kennelly poured himself a Scotch with soda and sat down in the living room.

Five minutes later Pipe walked through the living room and into the kitchen—stark naked. He poured himself a drink and brought it to the living room. "Excuse me," he said. "We are a pair of men, after all," Then he walked to the living-room closet and pulled out a robe. "Is there something we need to discuss?"

"I can't help but be curious about something," Kennelly said. "When I first talked with her, Eva Lee described you as a 'creep,' only interested in the fact that she had posed nude for Paul Weyrich. Two days later, not only does she crawl between the sheets with you but you give her an expensive diamond ring."

"*Crawl between . . . !* What makes you think . . . ?"

"Don't play games with me. I know you did. And I've seen the ring. What did that cost you, Rusty? Four hundred dollars?"

"Six. But so what?"

"Well, you weren't buying the tumble in the bed for six hundred dollars. There had to be something else involved."

Pipe slugged down his drink. "A minute," he said and went to the kitchen to pour himself another. He returned and sat down. "Captain Kennelly . . . Look at yourself. Look at me. You're an Irish lover type. I imagine you are loyal to your wife, but you don't have to be; a hundred women would tumble into bed with you. Then look at me . . . I . . . I try, but they don't like me. So Eva accepts me. I want to seal the relationship. I buy her an expensive ring. Can you find criminal intent in that?"

"Who said anything about criminal intent?" asked Kennelly.

"Well . . ."

"On the other hand, you do seem to have some odd friends. Let's start with Strecker."

"Only a friend. Only a man who extended friendship to a guy who was lost in Washington."

"Eva calls him a scary guy. She's afraid of him."

"Strecker? He's a little gruff, a bit too direct maybe."

"When did you see him last?"

"Oh, I don't know. It— Come to think of it, it was Saturday. That's when Eva met him."

"Did Julie meet him for the first time on Saturday?"

"I'm not sure. I guess she'd met him before. He was a friend of Paul's, too."

"Really?"

"Well . . . yes," said Pipe with the air of a man who has just disclosed something he wished he had not disclosed. "Paul came here as a young lawyer and started going to meetings of the District Bar Association: lunches and dinners, that sort of thing, to get acquainted. I think that's how he met Strecker. I *think* that's how it happened."

"How did *you* meet Strecker?"

"When you're doing what I'm doing, you meet a lot of

lawyers. They represent property owners who may be affected by your closing old drainage tunnels and so on."

"But your friendship is social now?"

Pipe nodded. "I guess we could call it that."

"You enjoy his company."

"Yes. I enjoy his company. Hey, he's a big guy. He was an officer in World War I. He's personable. And . . . Well, I guess I have to say he's the kind of man who influences others. And I have to figure he's the kind of guy who can do something for anybody he chooses to call a friend. You know? You meet some guys, sometimes, and you have to say, 'Hey, here's a guy that counts for something.' You want to make that guy your friend. It's not just that you figure he might do something for you. It's that . . . Hell, how can I explain it?"

XIII

TOMMY THOMPSON HANDED MRS. Roosevelt a memorandum received from a wartime agency, the Office of Censorship—

OFFICE OF CENSORSHIP

To: Mrs. Eleanor Roosevelt

To begin, we should like to say that many of us in this office fully enjoy your newspaper column "My Day" and never fail to read it. At the same time, however, we feel compelled to request a small alteration in it.

From time to time you make reference to the weather, as being cold or hot or rainy or snowy or windy, etc. Sometimes you do this when you are traveling with the President. These hints of what kind of weather you are experiencing can suggest to enemy agents where you and the President are. If, for example, you say it is a rainy day when it has not rained in Washington for a week, this tells anyone who reads your column that you are not in the capitol. A glance at a weather map may disclose to someone that you were either in New York or in Boston when you wrote the column, since those were the only cities experiencing rain during the past several days.

This office would greatly appreciate it if you would omit references to the weather from your column, for the duration of the war. We hope this will not seem petty or fanciful. From little snippets of information, great secrets are occasionally disclosed.

"You see?" she said to the President when she stopped during his cocktail hour and showed him the memo. "Our guardians are most meticulous."

He spoke to her in a low voice, so that no one else could hear. "I would be better satisfied with that if you could discover how Weyrich came to be in the Lincoln Bedroom with a gun on his person. I have to tell you, Babs, that one gets to me. Not much rattles me. That one does. Are you and your associates making any progress? I hope your answer is yes. For the first time in this war, I don't sleep easily."

"We are working quietly on it, Franklin. Isn't that how it has to be? Quietly?"

"Yes. So good luck with the Hawkshawing."

The First Lady went on out to a dinner for the wives of House Democrats.

Ed Kennelly was having dinner with his wife, at home, when the telephone rang.

It was Julie. "Eva is dead," she said in a voice dulled by horror.

"How? Where?"

"In our room. Strangled. The police are already here."

"Let me talk to the man in charge."

He arrived at the boardinghouse twenty minutes later and was stopped on the porch by Mrs. Bogardus who had fortified herself with whiskey and complained that "This is irreg'lar. I run a respectable house, and this kind of thing is irreg'lar."

Julie was sitting at the dining table, in shock. Two of the Government Girls were trying to comfort her. He spoke to her for a moment and then went upstairs.

Kennelly well remembered the room he and Stan had searched last Wednesday. He recalled a bright, cheery room on the front of the house, furnished chiefly with Victorian furniture, including one heavy oak bed in which the two young women had slept together.

The cheery room was a scene of ugly tragedy now. Eva lay on the floor at the foot of the bed, her body contorted by her death agony. It was plain that she had been strangled and possible that her neck had been broken.

Kennelly looked at the uniformed sergeant who had been in charge until now and shrugged.

The sergeant shook his head. "I've got no idea, Cap'n. No idea. That there wasn't done by the roommate. That there was done by a powerful man."

"When?"

"Say eight or nine. The medical examiner will be able to tell."

"Right . . ." Kennelly muttered.

He stared sadly at the crumpled little body, facedown on the floor. She had wanted to go home.

And—*Christ, Jesus!*—her ring was missing! The diamond ring given her by Rusty Pipe was not on her finger!

"How did the murderer get into this room?" Kennelly demanded of the sergeant. "The landlady doesn't let men come upstairs in this house. Somebody would have seen him on the stairs. This is a busy place."

The sergeant pointed to the window. "I figure there. Up a tree out front, over the porch roof, and in the window. It isn't locked. By eight o'clock it would have been dark. He could have made it, with luck. Then he just waited for her to come in."

Kennelly peered out the window. There was in fact a tree out there. "Take a pretty agile young fellow to climb up there and—"

The sergeant nodded. "Agile. Athletic."

"Which eliminates the man I would have had in mind," said Kennelly. Meaning Pipe.

"We're doing the standard things, Cap'n. Anything special you want done on this one?"

Kennelly shook his head. "Can't think of it. Uh . . . Keep in mind that she was a nice kid. No hooker, nothing like that. She didn't deserve this. *I want the ass of the man who did it.*"

He went downstairs to talk to Julie, who was crying and inconsolable.

"*Why*, Julie? Can you think of a reason?"

She sobbed and shook her head.

"You're mixed up with some pretty rough characters. Does it occur to you that you could be next?"

"What rough characters?" she whispered.

"*You tell me*," he grunted. "What I ought to do is put you back in the slammer, for your own protection. But I figure you maybe will get it through your head that these characters are not your friends. There's a girl lying on the floor up there that proves it."

He rang the bell, and Pipe came to the door.

"Figured you'd better get the word from me. Eva's dead. Murdered."

He wanted to see how Pipe would react to that news. The reaction was all that he could have asked for, and more. For a moment he thought the man was about to drop on his knees. Pipe shuddered. "*Oh . . . no!* My God, no!"

"May I come in?"

Pipe, who was wearing a robe, stepped back from the door and began to shake with sobs.

Kennelly was not sympathetic. He walked into the apartment and sat down on the couch. "Your diamond ring is missing. It was not on the body."

Pipe wailed.

"The time has come to quit playing games, kiddo. There ain't no fun left in this."

"*I didn't kill her!* When . . . ? I was on duty until just half an hour ago. Lots of men saw me. When . . . ?"

"No, you didn't kill her. But you know who did. Or, if you don't, you've got a pretty good idea who did. I myself got a pretty good idea who did. And why."

"Why, Captain? Why? Why would anyone kill a girl like that?"

"I got a better question," said Kennelly. "Why would anyone kill a guy like Weyrich. And, ol' buddy, I think you got a pretty good idea who did that, too."

"No! I don't know who did it!"

"You could be next, you know. You or Julie."

Pipe sobbed and shook his head. "I don't *know* who did it! Or why."

Stan Szczygiel came to Mrs. Roosevelt's study early Thursday morning. The morning newspapers carried the news of the murder of a young woman in a boarding-house. Kennelly had called and said he would be by shortly. In the meanwhile, the agent and the First Lady had other things to talk about.

"I've had several replies to my memo," he told her. "It turns out that Weyrich did indeed carry typewriters in and out of the White House. Which of course means he carried the pistol in here himself."

"And meant to kill someone with it," she said sadly. "And I'm afraid that who he meant to kill was the President. I must tell you, the President thinks so, too."

"But he never even tried, really," said Szczygiel.

"Do you suppose it's possible that he never meant to do it but was only delivering the pistol to someone else?"

"If that was the case, why did someone leave the pistol on him?"

"And why was the pistol wiped clean of fingerprints?" she asked.

Szczygiel shook his head and sipped appreciatively from the coffee she had ordered.

"None of which addresses the *big* questions," said Mrs. Roosevelt. "Who killed Mr. Weyrich? How did he get in here to do it? And why?"

"When we find out who killed Eva Lee, and why, we will have the answers to those questions," said Szczygiel. "I hope Ed—"

But of course Ed didn't know who killed Eva.

"Strangled," he said. "By big, powerful hands. Her larynx was crushed."

"For God's sake, *why?*" Szczygiel asked.

"She knew something," said Kennelly. "She knew too much."

"Then Julie . . . ?" asked Mrs. Roosevelt.

"I think she's in big danger. I've thought about locking her up again, until—"

"Bring her here," said the First Lady decisively. "We can put her up on the third floor and of the White House until—"

"Something more," said Kennelly. "We know that the Colt had been manhandled so much that fingerprints, even on its internal parts, were smudged to say the least. But I had the cartridges from the clip examined last night. Okay. Weyrich's fingerprints were on them. Which means—"

"Which means," said Mrs. Roosevelt, "that the pistol was not planted on his body after his death. *He loaded it.* And he was in the White House . . . But who killed him? And why?"

"Maybe the time has come to put some heat on Frances Schroeder," Szczygiel suggested.

Mrs. Roosevelt shrugged. "A formidable woman, they say."

"Mr. Szczygiel," said Frances Schroeder, "my husband was convicted of treason and died in a federal penitentiary. Is that not enough? What more does the Roosevelt administration demand of me?"

They sat in her office in her store. "Mrs. Schroeder, I don't represent the Roosevelt Administration. I am seventy-three years old. When I came to the White House, William McKinley was President. I retired, honorably. I was called back when many agents of our service entered the armed forces because of the war. I do have my political opinions, but I can say that officially I don't give a damn who is President of the United States. Do I have to recite the names of the Presidents I have served? William McKinley, Theodore Roosevelt, William Howard Taft, Woodrow Wilson, Warren Harding, Calvin Coolidge, Herbert Hoover, and Franklin D. Roosevelt. I imagine you liked some of them pretty well, Mrs. Schroeder."

"Franklin Roosevelt is—"

"*The President,*" Szczygiel interrupted. "Like it or not. And it is my job to see that no one assassinates him."

"Well, what do I have to do with that?"

"I hope nothing. I sincerely hope, nothing. I am sure, though, that you will do whatever you can to help me in my job."

"Like what?"

"My dear Mrs. Schroeder, you despise the President—for good reasons perhaps. I cannot and do not believe you wish his death by assassination. On the other hand, you may—through your well-known association with extreme anti-Roosevelt people and organizations—be able to suggest to me some investigatorial leads."

Frances Schroeder tapped her cigarette on the edge of a large ceramic ashtray filled with butts, that sat on her desk. She was dressed much the same as she had been the night the First Lady had met her: in dangling diamond earrings hanging below her stripped hair, in a clinging silk dress cut low enough to allow display of a diamond pendant necklace in her cleavage. Her desk was a leather-topped map table, and she had told Szczygiel immediately on his arrival that it had been used by General Robert E. Lee. The office otherwise was lavishly decorated with silk drapes, an oriental carpet, and paintings of race horses.

"Leads to an attempt to assassinate the President? Mr. Szczygiel, I despise this President, as you have suggested, but I am not an assassin."

"No, ma'am. I did not imagine you were. But someone has made an attempt on his life. Am I wrong in supposing you were acquainted with Paul Weyrich?"

"I never heard the name until I read in the paper that he was dead."

"Eva Lee?"

"Mr. Szczygiel, you name to me the names of people who have been murdered. I know nothing of this kind of thing."

"The hell she doesn't," said Szczygiel to Kennelly and Mrs. Roosevelt. "Does she think we are idiots? Does she think I'd ask her if she knew Paul Weyrich if I didn't know the answer? Isn't that the first rule of cross-examination that lawyers use? Never ask a question if you don't know the answer. We found a roll of film that Weyrich had exposed but hadn't developed. So we had those developed and printed. Look—"

Szczygiel spread on Mrs. Roosevelt's study table a dozen small photographs. They had been taken, apparently at a picnic, and each one showed Frances Schroeder grinning and drinking beer and presiding over the grilling of hotdogs. She wore a blouse and shorts—for once without the earrings and necklace—and was conspicuously sucking on a cigarette.

Standing beside her, with his arm around her waist, was a tall, fiftyish man. "Strecker, I bet," said Szczygiel.

"And what will you bet that somebody in these pictures is Dr. Lauder?" asked Kennelly. "Hey. This is a rogue's gallery of the potential—"

"Let us not leap to that conclusion too readily," said Mrs. Roosevelt.

"Oh. While we're at it," said Szczygiel, "let's not forget that the photographer here was Weyrich. If this was a picnic of the . . . Of the Klan. Whatever. He was there."

"When were these taken?" asked Mrs. Roosevelt. "Can anyone guess?"

"In picnic weather," said Szczygiel. "Either recently or last fall."

"Why do you suppose this roll had not been developed and printed before?"

"I have to guess. My guess is that Weyrich was an advanced amateur, a semi-pro photographer and gave big priority to his artistic photos. These are just snapshots, probably taken just to humor the crowd. He didn't care about them and left the film lying around undeveloped."

"Anyway," said Kennelly, "these snapshots prove that Frances Schroeder is a liar. She never heard of Weyrich until she read in the newspapers that he was dead, but she was chummy enough to pose for his camera, all smiles and skimpy shorts."

"I bet Eva was there, too. And Julie."

"Let's find out about Julie," said Mrs. Roosevelt. "I haven't told her yet that she will be invited to live in the White House for a little while. Maybe now is the time to tell her . . . and ask her a question or two."

Julie Finch arrived from the West Wing within ten minutes. She looked wan and shocked—and maybe a little afraid, as the First Lady judged.

She was wearing a print cotton dress, dark-blue and white, with a skirt shorter than the skirts Mrs. Roosevelt had seen on her before. She also wore the little gold cross on a chain that she had been wearing when the First Lady met her, and now she fiddled nervously with it. She wore no makeup, and her eyes were puffy, probably because she had been crying.

"Have a chair, Miss Finch. Be comfortable."

The young woman glanced at Kennelly and Szczygiel as she sat down. "I couldn't sleep in that room last night," she said in a quiet, shuddery voice. "I don't think Mrs. Bogardus is going to let me stay in the house anyway."

"We will solve that problem right now," said Mrs. Roosevelt. "We don't think you are safe there. I want you to move into a room on the third floor of the White House, until the murders of Mr. Weyrich and Miss Lee are solved."

"White House!"

"There are a number of nice rooms on the third floor. I'm afraid we can't put you in a suite, but you can have a bedroom with bath. The point is, you will be within White House security. If someone has a mind to do to you what they did to Miss Lee, you will be protected. Of course, this arrangement can't be permanent, but it can last until you no longer need protection."

"I 'preciate it. I 'preciate it more than I can say."

"Let me emphasize something to you," said Szczygiel. He spoke sternly. "Because you worked with Weyrich you learned some national security secrets. Now you are going to learn two more. General Dwight Eisenhower is living in a suite on the third floor. His driver is with him, occupying the second bedroom of the suite. That the general is in Washington is a deep secret. Also living up there is Miss Sarah Churchill. That she is in Washington suggests that someone else is in Washington—"

"The Pram Minister," said Julie. "I know *he's* here."

"Alright. And you also know that if you disclosed these secrets you would be subject to imprisonment at least for the duration of the war and maybe for a good deal longer. Clear?"

"Clear."

"I'll send two or three uniformed officers along to help you move your things out of the boardinghouse," said Kennelly.

"Miz Bogardus is gonna be so pleased."

"We have more things to discuss," said Mrs. Roosevelt. "Look at these photographs that were among Mr. Weyrich's effects."

Julie studied the pictures. "Sho," she said. "That's pictures of a picnic we had, over in Alexandria, last month."

" 'We,' " said Mrs. Roosevelt. "Who's 'we?' "

"Well . . . Paul and me were there. Mr. Strecker and Mrs. Schroeder. That's Mrs. Schroeder in the pictures. Her and Mr. Strecker are— You know . . ."

"Was Eva there?"

"No. Her an' Rusty were just kind of gettin' together then, an' he didn't want this crowd to see her yet."

" 'This crowd.' What crowd?"

"Well, these were folks that didn't like the President much."

"How about Dr. Lauder?"

"There was a man that was introduced to me as a doctor. I didn't get his name."

"Speak with a Southern accent?" asked Kennelly.

She nodded. "I s'pose you'd say that."

Mrs. Roosevelt had begun to peer at the photos through a magnifying glass. "What's this?" she asked. "What is that man doing?"

Julie squinted at the picture. "Oh, that's Mr. Strecker. He was chinning himself on that tree limb. He's a freak about that kind of stuff, wanted to prove he could chin himself I don't know how many times."

XIV

JULIE LEFT WITH KENNELLY, to go to her boarding-house and pick up her things. When they were gone, Mrs. Roosevelt was left alone with Szczygiel.

"I wonder about something," she said. "It seems to me that we have placed our confidence in the closing of tunnels and conduits in a man who now turns out to be a member of a Roosevelt-hating group. Could Major Pipe have opened an underground door for a killer?"

"I haven't pursued that possibility very far," said Szczygiel, "because frankly we of the Secret Service have never relied on anybody about this and have explored the understructure of this place on our own. In fact, we hired engineers to do it. Civilian engineers. What is more, we have added locks of our own to the doors the army has put in place."

"Even so," she said, "someone entered the White House, killed Mr. Weyrich, and departed."

"Either that or someone already inside did it."

"I shudder to think of that possibility," said the First Lady. "It would mean whoever did it is still in the White House and still a threat."

"My point is, Major Pipe is not the only one who has checked the tunnels and conduits under the White House grounds. I personally can't think of a way a person could get in and out."

"Are there blueprints?" she asked.

"Certainly."

"Can we go over them together?"

"Of course."

"I have a duty to perform first," she said.

The President left the Trident Conference for five minutes to be wheeled into the Rose Garden to present a plaque to another entertainer whose work for the USO and on bond drives had earned presidential recognition.

He was Jack Benny. Mary Livingstone was with him. As the cameras rolled and flashed, the President presented the plaque and then was wheeled away, back to the conference.

"The President," said Mrs. Roosevelt, "would have liked to remain here in the sunshine and spend an hour with you, Mr. Benny. Unfortunately, he is involved today in an important meeting that demands his presence and full attention."

"Of course," said Jack Benny. "I, too, have a sense of values and priorities . . . y' see. If I could be doing what he is doing, I wouldn't have time to chat with *me*. Where he has gone, I think, is where I wish I could go . . . down in the vault to visit *my money.*"

Flashbulbs flared, in spite of the sunlight, and the reporters and cameramen laughed—as did the First Lady, heartily.

"But Mary and I are deeply honored. I know that all of you are aware that Mary Livingstone is not really Mary Livingstone. She is in fact . . . Mrs. . . . *Jack* . . . *Benny*." He nodded and smiled as the members of the press corps applauded. "Actually . . . Actually, y' know, that's not completely accurate either. The fact is . . . Mary is . . . Mrs. . . . Benjamin . . . *Kubelsky.*" He waited through his exquisitely timed stage pause, then said, "And if you think *that's* bad, just remember, if she wasn't Mrs. Benjamin Kubelsky she might still be Miss Sadie Marks."

When Mrs. Roosevelt returned to her study, Stan Szczygiel was there with a large portfolio of blueprints. They showed the many tunnels and conduits that led into and out of the White House.

"This is the main electrical supply," he explained, pointing to two parallel lines that represented a tunnel. "The cables come through here. Later, when telephone lines were brought in, they laid them in the same tunnel. A man can walk through that tunnel—or could, except that both the Army Engineers and the Secret Service blocked it with heavy steel gates. Branching off from that tunnel are conduits that carry cables to various parts of the structure. A man can crawl on his belly through those—again, he could have before we installed gates. The army has keys to half the gates, and the Secret Service has keys to the rest. To get into the White House through these tunnels and conduits, you'd have to have keys from both services."

She put a finger on the blueprint. "I seem to remember that these are pedestrian tunnels, meant to be walked through."

"To the Treasury Department and the Old Executive Office Building. Those are open during the day, but people who walk through them go through security checkpoints and must show identification. They are also patted down for weapons. At night, barred gates are locked at both ends of those tunnels. Even then, there's a guard on duty at the White House end of each tunnel."

"These, Stan?"

"Those are the conduits for water and sewage pipes. An agile man could crawl through them, except again that they are blocked by locked steel gates."

"What is this?" she asked, pointing at a circle in the northeast corner of the building.

"That was a sump," he said. "There are two of them: one at the other end, too."

"Explain, please."

"The two sumps were almost certainly dug when the White House was built. You might think of them as dry wells. A primitive way of getting rid of household water. Kitchen water and bath water was poured down them and was supposed to be absorbed in the soil."

"Sewage?"

"No. Household water. They were not unusual in big houses in the eighteenth century. Instead of tossing the kitchen water and bath water out the door, you poured it down the sump. It soaked away in the soil and disappeared. Just household water. Nothing filthy."

"But . . . These lines?"

"After a good many years, accumulated soap and grease and coffee grounds, and the like, saturated the soil and made it less permeable. By then there was a system of storm sewers in the vicinity of the White House, so they dug tunnels to connect the sumps to the storm sewers. Old habits die hard, so for still more years they continued to pour buckets of water into the sumps. Eventually, of course . . . plumbing."

"So these ancient tunnels continue to afford access to the White House?"

"Except for one thing, ma'am. The sumps are twenty feet deep. To climb up or down one, a man would have to have a long ladder—and *that* you're not going to carry around in the White House."

"Can we view one of these?"

"Certainly."

The east sump was hidden under a curving stairway. It looked very much like a dug well. The stonework stood some two feet above the floor and was covered with a crude wooden lid. Szczygiel had picked up a powerful flashlight on the way and showed Mrs. Roosevelt that the sump was round, some four feet in diameter, and about twenty feet deep. A pile of rubble in the bottom showed how much stone had fallen from the walls over the century and a half, almost as long as the sump had been there.

"And that small archway opens, I suppose, into the tunnel to the storm sewer."

"Yes."

"Where is that blocked?"

"The old storm sewer itself is blocked with barred steel gates that let water through and prevent passage by persons. It has been that way for a long time, though the gates were reinforced in 1941."

"Why doesn't the rainwater from the storm sewer back up into the sump?"

"Because the storm sewer is deeper. The tunnel from the sump slopes down to the sewer."

The First Lady peered into the damp and gloomy depths of the stone-walled cylinder. "Tell me, Stan," she said. "Do you see anything unusual down there?"

Szczygiel shook his head. "Like what?" he asked.

"Well . . . does it seem to you that the stone rubble in the bottom is oddly piled? I mean, almost all the fallen stones are piled on the side of the sump opposite the tunnel entry, whereas the gaps in the stonework show that stone has fallen just about equally from the entire circumference of the shaft."

"As if somebody came through the tunnel and shoved everything out of his way," said Szczygiel.

"Exactly."

"Alright. Suppose someone has crawled through the

tunnel and is down in the bottom of the sump. How is he going to get up here?"

"I have to judge it would not be impossible for the right man," she said. "A man could wedge himself in there. Besides, so many stones have fallen that the gaps would give a climber purchase."

"It would take a young, strong, nimble man. Weyrich couldn't have done it."

"Why would he need to?" she asked. "He was already in the White House."

Szczygiel grinned. "Of course. I don't think Major Pipe could do it either."

"Must it have been a man? And must it have been just *one* person? This may be fanciful, but I have an image of a man standing in the bottom, maybe with a woman standing on his shoulders . . ." She shrugged. "Fanciful."

"Not altogether," said Szczygiel. "Not altogether. If Pipe got someone into the storm sewer . . ."

Mrs. Roosevelt sighed loudly. "It gets more complex and mysterious every day," she said. "Think of this: Mr. Weyrich brought a gun into the White House, presumably for the purpose of making an attempt on the life of the President. Presumably he was a member of a group of conspirators. Then why did someone kill him before he got his chance to make that attempt? We have identified only one group of possible conspirators. Were they working at cross-purposes? If so, why?"

"More questions without answers."

"Why can't we climb down there and have a look?" she asked.

"Oh, ma'am, I—"

"While you procure a ladder, I shall go dress in something more suitable for this little expedition."

In ten minutes they were together again at the sump. Mrs. Roosevelt was wearing her riding clothes: jodhpurs and a khaki shirt, her hair tied under a red bandana. Szczygiel had brought the ladder and had also changed into rugged slacks and a work shirt. Both of them had thought to bring along powerful flashlights.

He went down first. Then the First Lady came down the ladder. They stood and peered into the dark tunnel. The beams of light from their flashlights disclosed nothing but a dank shaft under the ground.

"No rats, I hope," she said.

"There would be, but all these passages are constantly seeded with rat poison."

"Well . . ."

Mrs. Roosevelt bent at the waist and bent her knees and moved into the tunnel. Moving in an uncomfortable crouch, she scrambled forward, brushing the damp walls to each side and dirtying her clothes with mud and mold.

They moved— She could not judge the distance, but it was not so much as fifty yards when they came to the barred steel gate Szczygiel had said would be there.

The lock was an oversize brass padlock, an antique.

They returned through the tunnel.

Standing at the bottom of the sump, Mrs. Roosevelt directed the beam of her flashlight at a metal object projecting from the stonework.

"Do you recognize that, Stan?" she asked.

"Uh . . . No, ma'am, I don't?"

"That's a piton: a mountain climber's piton."

They climbed the ladder and emerged from the sump.

"Stan . . . I'd like for you to do something. Mr. Strecker has complained bitterly that his German-speaking son-in-law is nothing but a prison-guard private in Texas. We know that Baum was a member of the German-American Bund. But is that the only reason why the army conspicuously doesn't trust him?

"Army Intelligence," said Szczygiel.

"Would you inquire of them, please?"

Returning to her study, Mrs. Roosevelt found a letter from Chicago, from Paul Weyrich's father—

May 17, 1943

Dear Mrs. Roosevelt,

I enclose a letter I received from my son only after I returned to Chicago. You will notice that it was mailed on the day of his death, that is to say on Tuesday, May 11. I left for Washington on Thursday, May 13 and did not arrive at home again until Sunday May 16. The letter came while I was away. In any case, I send it to you now, in the thought it may shed some light on the cause of Paul's death. I am sending this airmail so you may have it as soon as possible.

Sincerely yours,
Edwin Weyrich

The letter enclosed read—

May 10, 1943
Dear Dad,
By the time you receive this something very important may have happened, and I may no longer be of this world. I am going to try to contribute something very important to our country. If I succeed, I will be a hero. If I am killed trying, I will be a martyr.

It may also happen that I may lose my nerve and may back out. It is possible too that some hitch may develop and prevent my trying. In that case, please burn this letter and forget you ever received it.

When you know the quality of the men behind me, you will know how very right I was.

I will leave behind a political testament. It will be found on my person, no matter what happens to me. You will be able to read it. I believe you will be proud of me. Anyway, you will know I love you.

Sincerely,

Paul

Ed Kennelly returned, bringing Julie and her belongings back to the White House. Mrs. Roosevelt sent word to the third floor that she would like to see her. When Julie arrived, she showed her the letter Weyrich had written to his father. Julie frowned hard.

"Did you ever see that letter before?" the First Lady asked.

"No. Never."

"Do you see anything odd about it?"

Julie shook her head.

"Well, it was typed on *your* typewriter, not on his."

"Nothin' unusual about that. He used my typewriter sometimes. His was older and had some quirks—like sticky keys, letters out of line, and so on. For example, on his typewriter, the Remington, every time you typed an 'M' you had to reach up and pull the type bar back down. Since I did ninety-five percent of our typing, he let me use the good typewriter, the Underwood, and he used the old one. Sometimes, after I'd gone home for the day, he's sit at my desk and type stuff."

"We found none of his fingerprints on your typewriter."

"I don't s'pose you would. After I'd sat and typed on it all day, all the prints on it would be mine."

"Typed all day . . . ?"

"Sure. Look at the date on this letter. May 10. That's the day before he was killed. I'd guess he typed it that evenin' and left it to go out with the last mail on Tuesday. Well . . . By then I'd have typed all day Tuesday."

"Then his last personal letter to you—"

"Look at it. Dated Monday, May 10. I never looked at the type close, to see what typewriter it was typed on, but I bet you it was typed on my Underwood. That Monday night, after I'd gone, he sat down and wrote two emotional letters. They had to do with what he was plannin' to do on Tuesday night."

"I see. Well, you relax this evening. You can order dinner brought up from the kitchen. Or maybe you'd like to check with our two British guests who are also living on the third floor. They might ask you to join them for dinner."

Szczygiel and Kennelly had to walk through the President's cocktail hour to reach Mrs. Roosevelt's study. The President greeted them jovially but did not ask them to sit down.

The fact was, an unusual event was taking place: serious discussion was continuing during the hour when the President and Prime Minister liked to relax. The Allies had placed much emphasis and a good deal of confidence in a raid by British bombers on the dams that supplied electricity to the Ruhr. Trained aircrews had delivered special bombs that were designed to skip along the surface of the water behind the dams, then sink and explode against the underwater base of the dams. The mission was not to flood the Ruhr but to sharply curtail the electricity supply that supported the German armaments industry there. Now the report had arrived. Nineteen bombers had gone on the raid. Eight had been destroyed. Damage to the Ruhr dams was small.

Here was a disappointment.

In the First Lady's study, Szczygiel opened a small briefcase and pulled out a length of paper tape, held in loops by paper clips. The tape was yellow and three-quarters of an inch wide. The printing was in purple ink. It had come off a teletype ticker, the same as delivered stock quotations to brokers and sports scores to bookies. Szczygiel removed the paper clips and let the tape drop to the floor. Mrs. Roosevelt could read it and pass it over to Kennelly, sitting beside her.

XXQ . . . 44D6 . . . CONFIDENTIAL CONFIDENTIAL. DEPT. ARMY, COL. GEORGE HARRINGTON TO STANLISLAW SZCZYGIEL, UNITED STATES SECRET SERVICE, WHITE HOUSE. CONFIDENTIAL CONFIDENTIAL. PER YOUR REQUEST FIND HEREWITH SUMMARY OF FILE ON PRIVATE FREDERICK BAUM USA 15451786. PRIVATE BAUM IS REGARDED AS POOR SECURITY RISK AND HAS NOT BEEN CONSIDERED FOR COMMISSION OR ANY DUTY SIGNIFICANTLY INVOLVED IN NATIONAL SECURITY FOR REASONS AS FOLLOW. FIRST, PRIVATE BAUM WAS ACTIVE MEMBER OF GERMAN-AMERICAN BUND IN YEARS PRECEDING WAR.

SECOND, PRIVATE BAUM REMAINS OUTSPOKEN CRITIC OF UNITED STATES INVOLVEMENT IN WAR. THIRD, PRIVATE BAUM SPENT PROTRACTED VACATIONS IN EUROPE IN 1937, 1938, 1939, 1940, AND 1941. DURING THESE VACATIONS PRIVATE BAUM SPENT MANY WEEKS SKIING IN BAVARIAN ALPS AND CLIMBING LOCAL MOUNTAINS. DURING THESE TRIPS HE WAS SEVERAL TIMES SEEN IN THE COMPANY OF PROMINENT NAZIS INCLUDING ONE OTTO OHLENDORF WHO HAS BEEN IDENTIFIED AS A GENERAL OF THE SS. OHLENDORF HAS ALSO BEEN TENTATIVELY IDENTIFIED AS AN SS OFFICER RESPONSIBLE FOR THE EXTERMINATION OF JEWS. WITNESSES HAVE DESCRIBED THE BAUM-OHLENDORF RELATIONSHIP AS EXTREMELY CORDIAL. MRS. BAUM HAS BEEN DESCRIBED AS BEING MOST FRIENDLY WITH OHLENDORF AND FRAU OHLENDORF. THE BAUMS HAVE ALSO BEEN OBSERVED IN THE COMPANY OF DR. JOSEPH GOEBBELS. PRIVATE AND MRS. BAUM SPEAK FLUENT AND IDIOMATIC GERMAN. IT HAS BEEN CONSIDERED THAT IF PRIVATE BAUM WERE ASSIGNED TO INTELLIGENCE DUTY AS HAS BEEN URGED HE MIGHT WELL ELECT TO DEFECT OR WORSE TO SERVE AS A DOUBLE AGENT. THE BAUMS REMAIN IN INTIMATE CONTACT WITH THE AMERICA-FIRST ORGANIZATION AND OTHER ORGANIZATIONS INIMICAL TO THE WAR EFFORT. IN THE CIRCUMSTANCES, PRIVATE BAUM HAS BEEN ASSIGNED WHERE HE SEEMS LIKELY TO DO

LITTLE HARM—THAT IS—OUTSIDE THE WIRE AT A POW CAMP IN TEXAS. MRS. BAUM RESIDES WITH HER FATHER, ATTORNEY ROBERT STRECKER, IN ALEXANDRIA VIRGINIA AND VISITS PRIVATE STRECKER MONTHLY. END OF MESSAGE. CONFIDENTIAL CONFIDENTIAL.

"Are we to read into this that the army would rather have him *inside* the wire?" asked Mrs. Roosevelt.

XV

"I MUST ATTEND A dinner tonight," said Mrs. Roosevelt. "I must leave in about an hour. There is one more thing I would like to do before I go. I am most curious about the pitons in the sump."

Szczygiel ordered the ladder. The First Lady dressed while it was being obtained and carried to the sump. When she arrived, the ladder was already down in the shaft. Kennelly and Szczygiel were there, together with two Negro men who had carried the ladder to the east end of the ground floor.

All together they made a somewhat incongruous appearance: a lady dressed to the nines, in a summery white dress with white straw hat and white gloves, in the company of four men who had gathered at a hole underneath the stairway.

Kennelly had already climbed down and had come back up. "Very interesting," he told her. "What's down there is very interesting."

"What might that be?"

He took the flashlight from Szczygiel and directed its beam toward a metal object projecting from a crack in the stonework.

"I don't know the name of that thing, but—"

"That's a piton, Ed: a mountain climber's piton."

The piton was a heavy spike with an eye on the end. A climber would pound one into a crack, put a rope through it, and use the rope to climb as high as he could; after which he would reach up and pound in another piton and would continue the process, laboriously working his way up a stone surface.

"There are just three of them," said Kennelly. "The first one's about halfway up, then two more above that."

The First Lady led Kennelly and Szczygiel back along the center hall of the ground floor. She stopped in the elevator vestibule and spoke quietly.

"I believe this rather convincingly condemns Major Ross Pipe, does it not?" she asked. "He gave the climber access to the storm sewer and the drainage tunnel. I suppose there are others who could have done it, but he was intimately associated with a group who wished the President ill."

Kennelly shook his head. "The first piton's eight feet above the bottom."

"Meaning that someone stood on someone's shoulders," said Mrs. Roosevelt.

"A mountain climber," said Szczygiel.

"We are thinking along the same lines," she agreed. "Along the very same lines."

"Pipe—" Szczygiel began.

"He couldn't have climbed that shaft, pitons or no pitons," said Kennelly. "He's a little fella. Not strong. The man who climbed up the sump wall had to be strong."

"He could have been the one who stood on someone else's shoulder," said Szczygiel. "Little fella. He—"

"I should think," said Mrs. Roosevelt, "that even that would require a certain amount of agility, which we seem to agree doesn't belong to Major Pipe."

Kennelly shook his head and frowned. "I still can't imagine why someone entered into an elaborate scheme to sneak a gun into the White House and then murdered Weyrich before he could use it. He was *ready* to use it. He had made his way to the residence floor to use it. He had written final letters to his father and his lover. He—"

"I am beginning to think I *know* why he was murdered short of carrying out an attempt to assassinate the President—or the Prime Minister," said Mrs. Roosevelt.

"*Why?* For God's sake, why?" Kennelly demanded. "Explain it, *please!*"

"I had rather not give you my theory," she said. "Lest you adopt it as your own and close your minds to other possibilities. I have an idea. I am going to ask you to do two things, Stan. First, see to it that Julie Finch does not leave the White House. I don't think she'll try to leave, but if she does, don't let her."

"Is she a prisoner, then?"

The First Lady shrugged. "Why not? And one thing more, if she makes a telephone call, make sure we know who she called and . . . be sure someone listens to what she says and what is said to her. I dislike being an eavesdropper, but—"

The dinner she was committed to attend was actually a garden party with ample food in the form of hors d'oeuvres. It was held in the garden of the Brazilian Embassy but was sponsored by other Latin American embassies as well: Mexico, Argentina, Colombia, Chile. The purpose was to emphasize Latin American commitment to the wartime alliance often now referred to as the United Nations.

But for the Trident Conference the President himself would have attended. Besides Mrs. Roosevelt, the administration was represented by Secretary of State Cordell Hull, Secretary of the Treasury Henry Morgenthau—happily for the First Lady, since this meant that Elinor Morgenthau would also be there—and Nelson Rockefeller, Coordinator of the Office of Inter-American Affairs. A number of members of Congress were present, including Senator Harry Truman of Missouri.

Mrs. Roosevelt eschewed the liquor that was offered her and accepted only a glass of Tio Pepe, very dry Spanish sherry.

Having her friend Elinor Morgenthau there was a blessing, yet also awkward, since she must have been at pains not to seem so attached to Elinor that she avoided talking to anyone else. She was anxious, for example, to talk with Mrs. Truman, but the homey Midwestern woman was shy about approaching two figures she regarded as sophisticated aristocrats of the Hudson Valley.

The senator was not reticent. He approached with a great, honest smile and said, "I'm surely glad to see you, Mrs. Roosevelt. And you, too Mrs. Morgenthau. Has the missus come over to say hello?"

"Not yet, I'm afraid, Senator."

"I'll push her in your direction. She takes a lot of interest in gardening. Roses. She loves roses." He nodded at the meticulously tended rose beds in the embassy garden. "So do I. Only I've got an extra reason that most folks don't suspect. I love the smell of the little bit of fresh manure they put on the roses."

"So do I, Senator," said Mrs. Roosevelt, laughing.

When Truman had moved on, the First Lady told Elinor a story. "Someone is supposed to have said to Mrs. Truman, 'Can't you get the senator to say fertilizer instead of manure?' And Mrs. Truman is supposed to have said, '*I* thought it was a real accomplishment to get him to say manure.' "

Elinor laughed.

"I suspect the story is apocryphal," said Mrs. Roosevelt. "There is a tendency to make little jokes about Senator Truman. I myself suspect he is a better man than some people think. The President appreciates him, too."

"Who in the world is *that?*" Elinor asked, nodding circumspectly toward a dark-haired beauty across the garden.

"That," said Mrs. Roosevelt, "is Gene Tierney."

The actress was talking with Maxim Litvinov, People's Commissar for Foreign Affairs and now also Soviet Ambassador to the United States. In Washington, Litvinov and his English wife, Ivy, had become a pair of socialites. They rarely missed a party. At one time a trafficker in firearms for the Communist Party, he had spent time in jails and had been sent to Washington by Stalin because Stalin believed the United States was the only country in the world that could help him defeat Hitler; also that Litvinov could Americanize himself enough to be able to function as a diplomat in Washington.

Litvinov had arrived in the capitol in an ill-fitting, crudely tailored suit and had hied himself immediately to a tailor and haberdasher, asking to be outfitted as befitted an ambassador. Now conspicuously dapper, he was regarded as something of a fashion plate. The story was told that when he called on President Roosevelt to present his credentials, he was wearing some of his new clothes, and the President had asked him skeptically, "You get that suit in Moscow?"

Litvinov, accustomed to Moscow habits, drank heavily, but he exaggerated the amount of vodka he could hold—or underestimated its impact on him. He was often unsteady on his feet.

"Oh, God, look out," whispered Elinor Morgenthau. "Here comes that . . . Cissy Patterson."

Eleanor Medill "Cissy" Patterson was the owner of the Washington *Times-Herald*, two newspapers she had merged. She was related to Colonel Robert "Bertie" McCormick of the Chicago *Tribune*, and her paper was as sullenly anti-Roosevelt as the *Tribune*. It was redeemed by the fact that its deceitful journalism and hysterical editorializing were largely ignored by its readers who bought it for its social news and gossip—plus of course its comics and sports coverage. Cissy was in 1943, a bloated woman with skin that vaguely resembled the gin-blossom complexion of W. C. Fields. She was also a socialite with an extensive and costly wardrobe to which she devoted much money and attention.

"Mrs. Roosevelt! Mrs. Morgenthau! How nice to see you! Doing your bit for Inter-American amity, are you?"

"Our bit to win the war," said the First Lady.

Cissy Patterson laughed. It was not a genuine laugh; it was more a snicker. "Me, too," she said. "Got any news?"

"As a matter of fact, I just might have."

Elinor Morgenthau started with amazement when she heard the First Lady suggest that she might share the White House limousine with Cissy Patterson later that evening, that she might have an interesting news story for her.

"What have you done, Babs?" the President asked when the First Lady stopped by his bedroom the next morning. "Did you feed this story to someone at the *Times-Herald?*"

"I fed Cissy Patterson herself. I'd have fed it to Satan to get it run the way it is in the paper. Franklin, this

Weyrich thing is more serious than we thought, and it has to be cleared up."

The story, right-hand column, page one—

MYSTERIOUS GUEST IN WHITE HOUSE

A mysterious guest seems to have taken up residence in a third-floor guest room in the White House.

A witness apparently in an investigation into a possible conspiracy to assassinate the President, a former Executive Wing secretary is being held in "protective custody" in a comfortable room with access to the White House kitchen for her meals.

The identification of this young woman is being withheld by the Secret Service, but she is understood to be the former daughter-in-law of a member of Congress, who secured her a job in the White House.

The third floor of the White House has been the living quarters of some well-known people during the current administration. The late Louis McHenry Howe, political mentor and confidential adviser to the President lived there. Harry Hopkins and his wife have a suite there. Marguerite "Missy" LeHand, the President's private secretary for many years, had an apartment on the White House third floor.

Witness believed important

The Secret Service and others believe they have uncovered a widespread conspiracy, centered on former members of the German-American Bund and like organizations to assassinate President Franklin D. Roosevelt. The witness now being kept under cover is said to have indicated a willingness to disclose what she knows about this conspiracy and its members.

Those in charge of the investigation believe she knows a great deal. Indeed, her testimony may prove the key to swift police raids on the homes and offices of the alleged conspirators.

"Exactly how much truth is there in this story, Babs?" the President asked.

"Enough to bring the fox out of his hole," she said. "Or so I am hoping."

"Ma'am, am I a *prisoner?*" Julie asked tearfully.

The First Lady had come to the third floor to visit her. Julie had not been allowed to see the *Times-Herald* but knew she could not leave the third floor of the White House.

"I suppose you are, my dear," said Mrs. Roosevelt. "But it's a far more comfortable cell than the one you occupied in the District jail. Isn't it?"

Julie glanced around and nodded. The room was modestly but comfortably furnished, with a bed and night table, a bureau, a couch and coffee table, and several lamps. Adjoining was a bathroom. The door was not locked. She simply found herself blocked when she tried to go downstairs.

"Why?" she asked.

"You've lied to us. Consistently. You know a great deal more about the death of Mr. Weyrich and about what he was doing than you have chosen to tell. The results is that the President remains threatened by the people who killed Mr. Weyrich. Our country is at war. We can hold you indefinitely, under the special wartime powers of the presidency. But it won't be here. Remember the steel-barred cells you've occupied. You may live in one for the duration of the war and maybe longer. Unless you cooperate."

"And maybe even if I do," said Julie ruefully. "Mrs. Roosevelt—I am pregnant. I told you I might be. Is my baby . . . going to be born in prison?"

"Who is the father?"

"Paul. Paul Weyrich."

The First Lady sighed and shook her head. "You will be called upon," she said, "to give evidence. If you give it truthfully, you may win sympathy and leniency. I'll leave you to think about it."

Besides the investigation, Mrs. Roosevelt had much to demand her attention. She continued her column. American troops had invaded Attu, one of the Aleutian Islands of Alaska, which the Japanese had seized in 1942, just before the Battle of Midway. A Japanese dispatch reported that the Americans were using poison gas. Mrs. Roosevelt warned that the accusation could mean only one thing: that the Japanese were considering the use of poison gas themselves.

During the afternoon, Vice President Henry Wallace asked for an appointment. She saw him in her study.

"I can't get even a few minutes with the President right now. I know why, and I don't complain. But one of my people is being savaged by Martin Dies, and I need help."

Congressman Martin Dies was chairman of the House Un-American Activities Committee.

"I cannot but be sympathetic," said Mrs. Roosevelt.

Wallace's face was flushed. "A fake Nazi-hunter . . . a fake Communist-hunter . . . *a fake*, Eleanor, an egomaniacal headline-hunting fraud!"

The First Lady nodded. She did not disagree, but she was not going to say anything he could quote.

"I could have his *butt*, Eleanor. I have enough information on Dies to *jail* him, and the only reason I don't use it is that Frank specifically asked me not to stir up a political fuss. But right now he's after a young man who works for me in my economics office. And guess what Un-American activity the fellow has been involved in? He's a *nudist!* Before the war he went to some island in the Mediterranean and ran around buck-naked for a week's vacation. Silly, okay, but . . . an *Un-American activity?* A threat to national security? Dies is the threat. He and his ilk are a threat to everything we are fighting for!"

"I'll speak to the President about it," said Mrs. Roosevelt. "I don't know what he can do."

"Tell Martin Dies to go to hell is what he can do!"

"I think it might be wiser to slip your young man into another job," she said.

"Dies will run after whatever he thinks he can make into a headline. And this one is top-notch! Nudism!"

"A job in the private sector," said Mrs. Roosevelt. "With someone who can indeed tell Mr. Dies to go to . . ."

Wallace drew a deep breath. "I'd appreciate that, Eleanor. The awful thing is that Martin Dies doesn't know the young man from Adam and could care less if he runs around naked in some silly camp. But it makes *headlines!*"

"I'll let you know, Henry."

This Friday evening Mrs. Roosevelt decided to sit down with the conferees during the cocktail hour. She wondered if some of them—the Prime Minister in particular—didn't think it odd that she kept so much distance between herself and the men of what had to be the most important meeting going on in the world. Indeed, that is why she decided to accept the President's invitation to dinner. They would dine in the Private Dining Room.

It was a very rare occasion for another reason. She elected to accept and to sip charily from one of the President's favored cocktails: a martini. She knew that he had mixed them originally at three parts gin to one part vermouth. Then it had become five to one, then seven. It was a powerful potable, and she had even seen the eyes of her formidable mother-in-law glitter after drinking one. King George VI had drunk two in rather rapid succession during his visit to Hyde Park, after which the President had subtly discouraged him from taking another. For herself, she sipped sparingly. The martini was an acquired taste, but she had begun to acquire it and meant not to let it overpower her.

Winston Churchill did not acquire the taste. President Roosevelt had explained why—"In London, if you can get three tiny chips of ice in a drink you have accomplished something special. But a martini has *three* ingredients, not just two. Not just gin and Vermouth. Gin, Vermouth, and *plenty of ice.* The water from the melting ice is an essential ingredient. Without ice—water—the mixture of gin and vermouth is a menacing mixture."

Sarah Churchill had come down from the third floor for cocktails and dinner. Kay Summersby had not. She had learned that Julie Finch was not allowed to leave the third floor; and, never guessing why, had felt sympathy for the little Tennessee girl and had stayed with her for dinner. Sarah explained to Mrs. Roosevelt.

"Anyway, they've got a fifth of bourbon from Ike's kit, so they ought not to have too shabby a time."

• • •

Leaving the dinner as soon as she could without arousing suspicion, Mrs. Roosevelt hurried down to the ground floor and east to the stair hall and the sump.

A group of men stood around, shuffling nervously, silently waiting. Ed Kennelly was there. Stan Szcyzgiel. Three soldiers armed with rifles, under the command of Lieutenant Dugan, the officer who had witnessed the field-stripping of the .32 Colt. His .45 rode ominously his hip.

Officer Willoughby, the man who had found Weyrich, was there, together with another uniformed White House policeman.

"I asked for you, Mr. Willoughby," said Mrs. Roosevelt. "Since you were present for the first act, it seemed appropriate for you to be here for what we hope will be the last."

"Thank you, ma'am."

"It might be interesting," said the First Lady, "if Julie were here."

Szcyzgiel agreed and put in a telephone call.

Mrs. Roosevelt stared thoughtfully at the wooden lid of the sump. "Embarrassing if we're wrong," she said.

"Could happen *tomorrow* night," said Kennelly.

"No. I think the story I planted with the gullible Cissy compels them to make the attempt tonight.

"They've got a hell of a lot at stake," said Kennelly.

They waited.

Two Secret Service officers arrived with Julie in custody. She blanched when she saw where they were assembled. Tears ran down as she stared at the armed men surrounding the sump.

They waited longer.

About ten o'clock they began to hear sounds in the sump: subdued voices and grunts.

The party moved back.

Suddenly the lid was shoved off. A head appeared, then shoulders.

Julie screamed.

"Welcome to the White House, Mr. Strecker," said Stan Szczygiel as he flipped the switch that turned on lights and revealed the armed men with guns leveled at the man in the sump.

XVI

"OKAY. I'M ROBERT STRECKER. So what?"

Szczygiel shone his flashlight down the sump just in time to catch sight of a woman scrambling, into the tunnel. "The gate is closed and locked," he said. "You can come up or we can come down and get you."

Strecker was dressed in climbing gear, with various items attached to his belt. Among the items was a length of rope. He tossed an end down, the woman wrapped it around her right arm and gripped it with both hands. Strecker pulled her up. He was muscular, powerful, and lifted her with no great trouble.

"Marlene Baum, I presume," said Mrs. Roosevelt as the woman lifted herself over the rim of the sump and rose to her feet.

The woman nodded. Squat and husky, with a pinkish complexion, pale-blue eyes, and short-cropped blonde hair, she was surly and angry.

"Well! Mrs. R. You do indeed show up at odd times and

in odd places. So? We are trespassing," said Strecker. "We wanted to see the inside of the White House. I suppose you can send us to jail for breaking in like this, but—"

Lieutenant Dugan was behind Strecker and slipped off his back a double-strapped knapsack. The lieutenant opened the knapsack. Inside was a suit of clothes: lawyer clothes.

"Better if you were to be seen to look like a possible—" The first Lady paused. She had meant to say a possible British diplomat but stopped because she was not sure Strecker and Marlene Buam knew the British were in the White House.

The lieutenant relieved Strecker of his equipment, including an ice axe. Ed Kennelly and Mrs. Roosevelt exchanged glances. The ax had no doubt been used to drive the pitons into the stone wall of the sump, but it would equally well have shattered the skull of Paul Weyrich.

Strecker was six feet tall, maybe a little more. His face was deeply lined, and his head was balding and liver-spotted. But his face was stern, too, and he was the epitome of self-confidence, even in the circumstances he now faced. He glared at the team that had caught him intruding into the White House and seemed to defy them to make anything of it.

The White House police officers stepped behind him and cuffed his hands behind his back. Kennelly put handcuffs on Marlene Baum, allowing her to have her hands in front.

"You *bitch!*" she muttered at Julie Finch.

"I think it would be well," said Mrs. Roosevelt, "if we all sat down together and talked."

Other times, concluding investigations into other crimes, the First Lady had assembled people in the Cabinet Room. She did not want this crowd to walk past the room where the Trident Conference was still in session, so she had arranged a meeting around a big table in a workroom in the east end of the ground floor.

She had arranged for a stenographer with a stenotype machine to sit beside the head of the table, where Mrs. Roosevelt herself sat, presiding.

"This proceeding is entirely irregular, and any statements given will have no standing in a court of law," said Strecker. Because two soldiers stood behind him, his hands were cuffed in front now. "I want it on the record that I emphatically protest."

"Your protest is noted," said Mrs. Roosevelt.

The First Lady was flanked to the right and left by Ed Kennelly and Stan Szczygiel. Beside Kennelly was Major Ross Pipe, also handcuffed, and then Robert Strecker. Beside Szczygiel was Julie Finch and Marlene Baum. A little apart from the others, farther down the table, sat Lieutenant Dugan and Officer Willoughby. Soldiers and officers stood behind the participants, their backs to the walls.

The room was cluttered, its usual workaday furniture shoved back or removed to the hall. Half-empty paper cups sat on the windowsills and on the tops of wooden filing cabinets.

"What are you investigating anyway?" Strecker demanded. "We were caught inside the White House, where we weren't supposed to be. We admit it. And that's that."

"Not quite, I am afraid," said Mrs. Roosevelt. "What we are interested in is *why* you intruded into the White House in such a bizarre manner. You didn't come in to see the sights, Mr. Strecker. That's a feeble rationalization that is accepted by no one. Surely you can do better than that."

"If you've been listening to the bitch there," said Strecker, nodding toward Julie, "you may have it in mind that we came here to harm the President."

"One might believe many things about a man and woman who entered the White House the way you did. That evidence alone is enough to condemn you to a long term in prison."

Marlene Baum covered her hands with her face and shuddered, rattling the chain link between her handcuffs.

"Let's get one point out of the way," said Mrs. Roosevelt. "Major Pipe. You unlocked the gates in the storm sewer that allowed Mr. Strecker and Mrs. Baum to climb through the tunnel and enter the sump. Do you want to deny that?"

Pipe had been arrested while still on duty and was in a pair of fatigue coveralls, his oak leaves prominently displayed on his collar. He slumped in his chair and stared at the table. "I gave them keys," he muttered.

"When?" asked Mrs. Roosevelt.

"I'm not sure. Over a week ago."

"Why?"

Pipe raised his chin and looked at Strecker. "He asked for them."

"Asked . . . ?"

"Demanded."

"Urgently?"

Pipe nodded.

"Could that have been on Tuesday, May 11?"

"I suppose so. It could have been."

"And what else happened on Tuesday, May 11?" asked Mrs. Roosevelt.

"That's the day when Paul Weyrich was killed," Pipe murmured tearfully.

The First Lady nodded. "It was indeed."

She turned to Strecker and said, "The pitons weren't driven into the stonework tonight. You have made at least two visits to the White House, Mr. Strecker."

"Prove it," Strecker said defiantly.

"Why did you come here tonight?" Kennelly asked gruffly.

Strecker shrugged. "To stroll through the rooms and see the beautiful furniture."

Mrs. Roosevelt handed the front page of the Washington *Times-Herald* to Julie Finch. "Read that," she said. "Then you'll know why he came here tonight."

"*You planted that story!*" Strecker blurted. "By God, you planted it!"

The First Lady smiled faintly. "To use a phrase of which *you* seem to be fond, so what?" She turned toward Julie. "You see, my dear, he came here to *kill you.*"

Julie glared at Strecker. "You did! You *bastard!* And you killed Eva!"

Strecker shook his head. "I seem to be dealing with hysterical people."

"People tend to become hysterical," said Mrs. Roosevelt, "when they discover that someone means to murder them."

"Well, no one's dead," Strecker grumbled.

"Correction," said the First Lady. "Two people are dead. Mr. Paul Weyrich and Miss Eva Lee. In time—" She paused and glanced at Julie and Pipe. "—Miss Finch and Major Pipe might have been killed, as you eliminated one witness after another."

"I never heard of anybody called Eva Lee!"

"You spent an hour with her in Major Pipe's apartment on Saturday afternoon. I can't prove right now that you killed her, but I believe I can prove you killed Paul Weyrich."

"Am I to understand—?"

"Yes," Kennelly interrupted. "You are under arrest for murder."

"We'll see about that!"

Mrs. Roosevelt turned to Pipe and Julie. "Both of you are in big trouble," she said. "You face—" She shook her head. "—major prison terms. You can help yourselves by cooperating."

"Let's rehearse a ridiculous scenario," said Strecker. "I am supposed to climb out of the sump, find my way through the White House, evading all the guards, and make my way to the third floor. And there I am supposed to kill . . . *that one.* Hell, I've never been in the White House before! I couldn't have made it out of this basement—"

"Then why did you come?" Mrs. Roosevelt asked coldly. "Why did you choose this curious way of gaining entry? You're a prominent lawyer. You could have asked for a tour of the White House, and it would have been granted. Someone would have guided you through all the rooms."

"Okay, and without a guide I would have been completely lost."

"No, you wouldn't," said Julie in a quiet, accusatorial voice. "You wouldn't have been lost at all." She turned and spoke to the First Lady. "I don't know if he's ever been in the White House before, but I know he wouldn't have been lost. He knows every room, every hall, every stairway. He's studied blueprints of the floor plans. Studied them? He knows them like the back of his hand."

"Where did he get such plans?" asked Mrs. Roosevelt.

"From Dr. Lauder. I don't know where *he* got them."

"Why?" asked Kennelly. "Why did he want those plans?"

Julie fastened a brittle, angry gaze on Strecker. "He *rehearsed* Paul. Bob Strecker is not the kind of man who leaves anything to chance. They worked and worked together. He knew where Paul was going to go, how he was going to evade the guards, how he was going to get to the President. Paul had to come into the residential area and study the movements of the White House police, then report all that to Bob. They worked on it and worked on it: every last detail of the plan."

"You are confessing," said Mrs. Roosevelt solemnly, "that you *knew* Mr. Weyrich planned to assassinate the President."

Julie wiped her eyes with the backs of both hands. "You've had that figured out for a long time," she whispered.

"Her word—" Strecker started to say.

"Against yours," Kennelly interrupted. "The Virginia police are executing a search warrant for your home. The DC police are executing one for your office. If we find those blueprints—"

"There could be all kinds of reasons for my having them," said Strecker. "Historical interest."

"Coincidence," Kennelly sneered.

"Alright, Mr. Smart Detective. I believe you police people look for several elements when you try to find and convict a murderer. I believe one of those elements is *motive*. Let's suppose I involved myself in a conspiracy to assassinate the President. Let's suppose I worked with Weyrich on it. Let's suppose I rehearsed him on the when and how. Let's suppose all that. Then why, in the name of God, would I break into the White House at great risk on the night when he was supposed to do it—and kill him?"

"That has been the chief question on my mind, Mr. Strecker," said the First Lady. "Assuming all your suppositions, why would you?"

Strecker twisted his face in a mocking leer. "You answer the question, Mrs. Roosevelt. Let me hear your answer."

"I have one, Mr. Strecker," she said. "I am afraid it involves . . . untruths told us by Julie Finch."

"She is going to make a beautiful witness," Strecker said scornfully.

"She doesn't have to," said Mrs. Roosevelt. "Let us look at photostats of some documents. First, here is a letter written by Mr. Weyrich to Miss Finch—"

> Dear Julie,
> Would you pay me the ~~honnor~~ honor of allowing me to take you to dinner this evening? If not this evening, then tomorrow evening? Please say yes.

"Another—"

> My very darling Julie,
> A word of thank~~e~~s for last night. Not of~~f~~ten in his whole life does a man meet a girl so loving and ~~carrying~~ caring. You are truly my ~~Valantine~~ Valentine.

```
Dearest,
Being with you is true ~~hevven~~ heaven. We
have got to do some thinking just the
same. I'm not sure what would happen to
us if it got around that we ~~meean~~ mean so
much to each other. I hope you haven't
spoken to anybody about us. Don't forget
that if I lost my job here I would prob-
ably be drafted, and we don't either one
of us want that. I'll see you tonight,
but be carefull!
```

Mrs. Roosevelt smiled.

"Apart from a fault in his typewriter that cause his letters 'u' to go askew, it is apparent that Mr. Weyrich was not a skilled typist. Then he wrote a letter to his father. Look at this—"

```
May 10, 1943
Dear Dad,
By the time you receive this something
very important may have happened, and I
may no longer be of this world. I am
going to try to contribute something
very important to our country. If I suc-
ceed, I will be a hero. If I am killed
trying, I will be a martyr.
  It may also happen that I may lose my
nerve and may back out. It is possible
```

too that some hitch may develop and prevent my trying. In that case, please burn this letter and forget you ever received it.

When you know the quality of the men behind me, you will know how very right I was.

I will leave behind a political testament. It will be found on my person, no matter what happens to me. You will be able to read it. I believe you will be proud of me. Anyway, you will know I love you.

"Not a single typographical error," said Mrs. Roosevelt. "Julie—Paul Weyrich didn't type the letter to his father, did he?"

Julie shook her head.

Marlene Baum burst into tears. She shoved her handcuffed hands toward her father. "The rest of my life, Dad!" she sobbed. "The rest of my goddamned life!"

Strecker shook his head convulsively. "Courage, Marlene," he muttered. "The cause is worthy."

Mrs. Roosevelt turned toward Julie. "In his letter to his father he spoke of a 'political testament.' What was that?"

"I can't recite it," said Julie, "but it was about what he was goin' to do and why he was doin' it. He said . . . the good of the world required the death of Franklin D. Roosevelt."

"*Bitch!*" grunted Strecker.

"And what did you do about that, after you typed it?" asked Mrs. Roosevelt.

"I begged him to tear it up and forget it," Julie sobbed. "It said too much, and if it got found after somethin' went wrong— He said it was his last will and testament. If he didn't leave a document like that, he said, people would think he was a stupid fool like the men who killed Lincoln and Garfield and McKinley. He wanted it understood that he did what he did as a reasonable man with good reasons, in association with respected people."

"When he wouldn't destroy it, you—"

"I called *him*," she said, pointing at Strecker. "I told him about the political testament. It could hang all of us. I was still trying to get it away from him when we were in the Red Room."

Mrs. Roosevelt nodded at Strecker. "So . . . Using the key provided you by Major Pipe, you entered the storm sewer, crawled through the tunnel to the sump, and climbed out of the sump. In this you were assisted by your daughter Marlene. You changed into clothes that would not be conspicuous in the White House and made your way to the Lincoln Bedroom."

"Why the Lincoln Bedroom?" Kennelly asked.

"Because it was empty," said Julie. She paused. "Look. Here's the way it was. All these people had somethin' in common. I mean, Strecker and Marlene, Dr. Lauder and Mrs. Schroeder, and a bunch of others. They hated President Roosevelt. I mean, they *despised* him. They sat around and talked about how too bad it was they couldn't do somethin' about him. The were terrible frustrated. This is before I get in the picture, understand."

"Understood, of course," said Mrs. Roosevelt.

"Then somethin' happens. Along comes Paul. He was from Chicago and had grown up with the *Tribune* shoved down his throat every day—"

"His father has worked for the Chicago *Tribune* all his life and is a personal friend of Colonel McCormick," said the First Lady. "One of his two brothers also works for the paper."

Julie nodded. "Me, I didn't know nothin' about the Chicago *Tribune*, but once I got workin' for Paul I got it shoved at me . . . till I got to understand how much that nasty old man McCormick hated the President."

"Which leads us to where, Julie?"

"Great good luck for Strecker and his friends. Paul was lonesome in Washington and took to goin' to lawyer meetings to meet people. He hears talk. He gets acquainted. And suddenly Strecker's got a man workin' in the White House who hates the President almost as much as he does. Then another piece of luck. Paul has a friend in the army who works at blocking ways to break into government buildings by comin' through tunnels and like that. So . . . They worked on these two guys, recruited 'em as you might say."

"Do *any* of you believe her?" Strecker asked.

"It didn't take much," Julie went on. "Paul was smart, but there was a limit to his smarts. Rusty's smart, but he's got his limits, too. The problem for Strecker was that neither one of 'em, Paul or Rusty, had any real experience with girls. I was nice to Paul, an' he fell for me hook, line, and sinker. Eva was a little nice to Rusty, an' *he* fell for *her*. Pretty soon, Paul told me what he was mixed up in; and not long after, Rusty told Eva."

"Why?"

"To make themselves look like big guys. All their lives those guys had been losers with girls."

"They made a big problem for Mr. Strecker," said Mrs. Roosevelt.

"Right. They could drop the whole project or they could take us in on it."

"Why," Szczygiel asked solemnly, "would you lend yourself to a scheme to assassinate the President of the United States?"

"Tard of bein' a loser," she said. "Tard of bein' *nobody*."

"A hell of a distinction to seek," said Kennelly.

"I never wuz too bright. Maybe in the slammer they can teach me somethin'," she said sarcastically.

"Why the Lincoln Bedroom?" Kennelly asked again.

"Like I said, because it was empty. The point was to have a room where Paul could open the door a crack now and then and see what was happening on the second floor. The point was that the conference would break up, and then the President and the Prime Minister would come up and go to bed. The Lincoln Bedroom suited. But it had got empty only the day before, when General Eisenhower had asked for a suite on the third floor, instead of the Lincoln Bedroom. That fouled things up for our guys. Eisenhower was assigned to the room where Paul had expected to hide. Y' see, he could slip down the stairs from there, peek out, then go back up."

"Cockamamie notion," grunted Kennelly—using a faddish word that had come into the language only in the past two or three years. "The idea he could get from anywhere on the second floor to the President's bedroom and—"

"There was an alternative plan," said Julie. "If he saw he could not get to the President, then he would kill the Prime Minister. Strecker thought that would be so damaging to the Roosevelt name that he would resign, or at least not run for a fourth term next year."

"Tell me," said Mrs. Roosevelt. "If Mr. Weyrich had succeeded in killing the President or Mr. Churchill and had been able to flee the scene, how did he expect to escape from the White House? Through the sump and so on?"

"It was to have been Paul's escape route," muttered Pipe.

"Except that down there he'd of run into Strecker and died soon and quick," said Julie. "I'd figured that out. I warned him about it when we were in the Red Room. But, like I already told ya, Paul was not too bright—not about people, anyways."

"We now know why the body was turned over," said Kennelly. "So the killer could get the 'political testament' out of Weyrich's inside pocket. Strecker . . . You killed Weyrich to get that piece of paper off him."

"Prove it," Strecker mumbled.

"The autopsy crew very carefully measured the wound to the head that killed Paul Weyrich," said Kennelly. "What would you like to bet that the wound measures exactly the same as the blunt end of the ice ax that you were carrying tonight?"

XVII

THE WOUND MATCHED THE ax. The accumulated evidence resulted in a quick conviction.

On Wednesday, September 15, 1943 Robert Strecker was hanged on a gallows temporarily erected in the Navy Yard.

Marlene Baum was sentenced to life imprisonment and was in the Federal Women's Reformatory at Alderson, West Virginia when her father was executed. Her husband divorced her in 1946, on the ground that she was an imprisoned felon. In 1951 she escaped and was at large for three weeks before she was recaptured. During her weeks at large she committed an armed robbery. She died in the reformatory on January 11, 1983, at the age of sixty-eight.

Ross T. Pipe was sentenced to life imprisonment and sent to Leavenworth, from which he was paroled in 1961.

Julie Finch received leniency because she had ultimately cooperated in the investigation and because she was pregnant. She was sentenced to twenty years imprisonment but received a commutation of sentence from President Truman in 1951, on the recommendation of Mrs. Roosevelt. A son was born to her at Alderson and was placed in the custody of Congressman and Mrs. Lawrence Mellon, who were already rearing her daughter by their son.

The congressman and his wife lived in Georgetown. Lawrence Mellon Jr., Julie's former husband, moved in with them after his discharge from the navy. He began driving to Alderson once a month to visit Julie. When she was released, they remarried. He was working as an automobile salesman in Washington, and they decided to stay there and establish a home for their two children. During her eight years in the reformatory Julie had been taught to sew. She took an interest in making her own clothes, later in designing them. By 1956 the clothes she designed and made were enough admired that she opened a small couturier shop and made clothes on a bespoke basis. The shop prospered. Soon she had a small business with six employees.

They had taught her something more at Alderson: to speak grammatical English. Mademoiselle Julie, as she called herself, spoke correctly and without an accent.

In 1960 she went to New York to present a dinner dress to Mrs. Roosevelt.

Frances Schroeder was arrested and held in the District jail as an accessory to the plot to assassinate the President. She testified at Strecker's trial that he had talked grimly of a plan to kill Franklin Roosevelt but that she had taken it for bravura and nothing more. After his conviction, she was released, and the charges were dropped.

The Cross-Channel Invasion promised for May, 1944, occurred on June 6, 1944. Called Operation Overlord, its supreme commander was General Dwight Eisenhower. The disappointed General George Marshall remained Chief of Staff, United States Army. The disappointed General Sir Alan Brooke remained Chief of the Imperial General Staff and was created First Viscount Alanbrooke.

Kay Summersby remained General Eisenhower's driver for the remainder of the war and afterward wrote a book in which she described their relationship as one of the mutual confidence and affection but one that did not involve intimacy. Sarah Churchill returned to her career as an actress and appeared in several motion pictures.

On the day when Robert Strecker was hanged, Mrs. Roosevelt was on Guadalcanal, visiting the tent hospitals where American servicemen were recuperating from wounds. An air-raid alarm sounded, and she was hurried into a sandbag shelter. But no Japanese bombers appeared that day.